Ghostly
Tales of
Iowa

Dedication from Ruth:

To my father, Reverend William Ullerich; my mother, Emma Ullerich (who would be surprised that I wrote these stories); and my native state of Iowa.

Dedication from Vicki:

To my parents, Dick and Bev Hinsenbrock.
To my nieces, Kelly, Kara, and Stacy, and their mother, my sister, Kim. To my great niece, Brooke.
To my husband, Charlie, who puts up with my clutter and my books and loves me all the same.
And to David W., Carl B., and Alan K., who all left this world much too soon.

In some instances, names and locations have been changed at the request of sources.

Content Warning: This book contains several references to suicide and may not be appropriate for all audiences.

Cover design by Travis Bryant and Scott McGrew
Text design by Karla Linder
Edited by Emily Beaumont

All images copyrighted.
Images used under license from Shutterstock.com:
Covers and silhouettes: **Elena Pimonova:** bat and tree;
sollalexta: branches

First Edition published by Iowa State University Press in Ames, Iowa, in 1996.

10 9 8 7 6 5 4 3 2 1
Ghostly Tales of Iowa
Second Edition 2005
Third Edition 2022
Copyright © 2005 and 2022 by Ruth D. Hein
and Vicki L. Hinsenbrock
Published by Adventure Publications
310 Garfield Street South
Cambridge, Minnesota 55008
(800) 678-7006
www.adventurepublications.net
All rights reserved
Printed in the U.S.A.
ISBN 978-1-64755-303-6 (pbk.); eISBN 978-1-64755-304-3

Ghostly Tales of Iowa

Ruth D. Hein and
Vicky L. Hinsenbrock

PUBLICATIONS
Adventure

Table of Contents

Acknowledgments

Thanks to all who responded to our requests for ghost stories from Iowa. The time you took to tell us about your experiences and to answer our questions made the book possible. Thanks also to friends and relatives for helping us find stories.

With generous help from librarians and historical society personnel, we researched settings and backgrounds for the stories in documents, newspapers, and other publications. In some cases, names and locations are disguised to respect the wishes of the storygivers.

Preface

The stories in this book came from different people and places in Iowa. Many are from northeast Iowa because some of them were published in our earlier book, *Ghostly Tales of Northeast Iowa* (1988).

Iowans were willing and, in fact, eager to share their stories with us, so that we could share them with our readers. Some of the stories are well known—for example, those connected with the house outside Guttenberg, or Lawther Hall and the Strayer-Wood Theater on the UNI campus in Cedar Falls. But others are stories that have been handed down through generations from grandparents and great-grandparents. And some happened in the last few years.

We hope you enjoy these new and old Iowa ghost stories. Some will give you chills; some will make you laugh. But all have a place in Iowa's history of storytelling.

Barney's Still Around

It was opening night at The Landmark. Everything was in order. Dick and Diane had worked hard to ready their supper club for this night. After the remodeling was completed, finishing touches were added: old photos, an old-fashioned wall telephone, an antique buffet, "railroad chairs," and other items reminiscent of the early years when the building had been known as The Landmark Inn.

When they heard car doors closing and people coming in the front door, Dick and Diane went downstairs to welcome their guests. Dick stopped off at the kitchen first to check whether the cooks were ready. Diane took one last look around the dining area before she went to greet a group of customers off to one side of the room. After several well-deserved compliments on how inviting the atmosphere was, someone asked her, "Has anything happened yet?"

Diane's first impulse was to answer, "Well, yes! We've changed the building a lot, put gobs of money and work into it—can't you see the difference?" when a loud noise made it unnecessary for her to answer at all. The noise came from upstairs, where Dick and Diane's living quarters were. It sounded as though something quite heavy had fallen to the floor up there. A couple of customers' smiles faded.

Diane excused herself to go back upstairs. As she went up, she thought, *No one is supposed to be up here!* What she found was the large photo of her parents not on the bedside table, but on the floor. It was mostly intact; just a small corner of the glass was chipped. But she knew that the photo had been placed so that it could not fall off by itself. Realizing its cast iron frame made it so heavy that it made the loud noise, she put it back and went downstairs.

As she rejoined the group, one woman asked a bit hesitantly, "Um...was it Barney?"

This group of customers and others who had lived in the area for a long time knew the history of the building. They had read about it in *The History of Allamakee County* and in the book *Past and Present of Allamakee County*. They knew that the main house was built in 1851 as a private residence by Colonel John A. Wakefield. At a very young age he had been a scout in the War of 1812. Wakefield then studied medicine and law and was admitted to the bar in 1818. He enlisted in the army and fought in The Blackhawk Indian War. Afterward, he served as a judge in St. Paul before moving to Allamakee County in northeast Iowa. He apparently was given the land on Lansing Ridge in 1851, and on it he built the grand, two-story house.

Under changing ownership, the building had later housed a brewery, a hotel and residence, a tearoom and restaurant, a general store, a post office, a bar, a gas station, and a dance hall before it had become and remained a restaurant.

They knew about the waitress who had seen Barney during a previous ownership. They knew he had been around for a long time.

Many years ago, when an old stage road went by there, the stagecoach stop was up the road about a mile, near the three-story, hand-built, rock school named the Lycurgus School. Back in the days when passengers, the mail, and other important cargo went by stagecoach to various destinations, passengers often stayed at the Landmark Inn for the night.

When one of the succession of owners operated a brewery in the building, drivers and teamsters found it an ideal place to visit while their horses rested. The men often spent the evening enjoying food and drink before their next run. Sometimes the natural competitiveness already present among them, augmented by a few drinks, led to arguments as to who was the better driver—or the faster driver—or who had the fastest horses or the smoothest-riding rig.

Late one night, when most of the weary travelers had slaked their thirst and had retired to their rooms upstairs at the inn, the arguments developed into a fight on the lower level. This resulted in the death of a teamster named Barney Leavy. That's about all anyone knows about it now, except that later owners claim that Barney's ghost still haunts the place.

Diane recalled the many questions asked of them while they worked at the remodeling. She knew that the story about Barney had been perpetuated over the years. She could add to the story, if she felt so inclined. She could tell about the strange noises and flickering lights in the old building when they first came to it. A light in the kitchen often came back on after they had turned it off. And she remembered something that happened just once when they were first remodeling the building. It was in the middle of winter. They were working in the main dining room. When they locked up at night, everything was okay. But when they came back the next morning, there was a big pool of water on the floor in the middle of the room. She said, "There's a second floor, so it wasn't a leaky roof. And there was snow on the ground at the time, but we didn't find any tracks outside. And we checked the locks. They were all right. At the time, Dick looked at me sort of funny and he said, 'Barney?'"

So Barney must still be around. If you want to meet him, you'll find the former inn, now called The Landmark, on State Highway 9 between Waukon and Lansing about a mile and a half from Churchtown in northeast Iowa. Diane and Dick Prestemon operate it as a supper club—one with a past.

The Cellar Witch

Clayton County in northeast Iowa was settled largely by German immigrants. Most of these were thrifty, hard-working, sensible farmers from the "old country." But even these practical folks had ghostly stories.

A young lady and her parents had come to America when she was a small child. As she grew older, Clara wanted to be out on her own more. Clara's mother had warned her several times not to dawdle on her way to and from town. Her mother especially warned Clara and her sisters to stay away from a certain house in town, vacant now but rumored to have been lived in by a witch. Many people believed the witch's spirit still resided in the house.

Clara knew she shouldn't, but several times she had driven by the house with the horse and buggy, always in the daylight. She secretly was just a little scared but enjoyed both the tiny shiver of fear and the knowledge of her disobedience.

One cool fall day Clara's parents sent her to town close to chore time to get various things from the general store. There were several customers ahead of her and she got to talking to Otto, a neighbor boy about her age. When she finally picked up her packages and loaded them into the buggy, the sun was just starting to drop behind the heavily wooded hillside. She set the horse to an easy trot and headed for home.

Without her really planning it, she was suddenly near the house. The big, two-story home had many windows, and the last rays of the sun reflected a wavy red in the handmade glass panes. Brush obscured the porch to one side, but no brush or grass grew around the front of the house. Clara could clearly see the row of basement windows and the outside, almost flat entrance leading down into the limestone foundation.

Some force made Clara stop the buggy and get out. The wind picked up and the horse was restless, stamping and whinnying. An old iron fence with a series of spiked tops surrounded the house. Clara approached slowly, eyes fastened on the shining red windows and especially the lower basement windows, turning from red to black as the sun continued to drop. Her hand touched the gate, which looked rusty and felt very cold. It swung open smoothly and quietly, no sound coming from the rusty hinges. Clara hesitated. Everything she knew and believed told her to stop, but she seemed unable to control her body. She walked through, toward the basement door. Vaguely, she could hear the horse running away. She stood above the basement entrance and closed her eyes. In that instant, she knew if she lifted the door to the basement, she would never come back.

Without warning, a strong arm pulled her back, dragging her away from the house. She felt as if pulled in two, a force pulling her back to the house and a powerful body pulling her away. The body yelled several times, and then the force let go. When she opened her eyes, she was on the street again, the gate shut, the house completely dark, and the wind blowing stronger still, like the beginnings of the tornado they'd had last year.

Looking up, Clara saw Otto kneeling beside her. Speaking in German, he asked her if she was hurt. She slowly shook her head from side to side.

"Why did you come? What happened?" she asked.

Looking less frightened, Otto spoke in English this time. "I was following you to be sure you came home safely. When your horse ran past me, I knew you had trouble. I came to look and found you standing here, about to go in. Why were you here? It is a dangerous place for you."

Clara looked down, embarrassed. "I don't really know. I—well, I've driven by here before and I just found myself here."

"Do you know the story about the witch?" Otto asked.

"I know my parents told me to stay away and said there was a witch who used to live here."

"Come to my wagon. I will tell you the story."

Otto helped her stand up and walked her to his wagon. Once there, he resumed his story. "The woman who lived here before was dreadfully afraid to die. My parents say she was a witch, but even witches can die. She wanted to live forever. But the only way she could keep on living was to find another body, since hers was worn out and old."

Clara shuddered. "Is she still there?"

Otto looked at her solemnly and continued. "Many years ago, she did finally die. Since then she has been looking for a body. She tries to lure young girls to her basement. If she can get a young girl to come to her basement, she will take her body and be young again. That is why parents tell their daughters to stay away. I could help you because she does not want men."

Clara knew the reason for her feeling now. The feeling that told her if she went into the basement she would be lost forever. She smiled weakly at Otto as she said, "Let's go home. I promise I will never come here again."

Charley's Ghost

Charley's ghost wasn't really Charley's ghost—rather, it wasn't the ghost of Charley. But because it was Charley Nelson and his family who were most affected by the phenomenon, it came to be referred to as "Charley's ghost."

The Nelsons had come up to Iowa County from the South in about 1923, according to Jess Bean of Williamsburg. The family consisted of Charley; his wife; their son, Gordon, who was Jess's age; and their daughter, Mary, who was four or five years older than Gordon.

Charley's job was to shovel coal into raised hoppers for the steam engines on the railroad. That's why they lived in a remodeled boxcar that sat across from the depot. Except for a crawl space under it, it sat right on the ground, without any wheels. There was a door at each end for easy entrance and exit.

Jess Bean was 9 or 10 then. He and Gordon Nelson were pals, and their fathers became acquainted too. Jess's father, William T. Bean, was the security guard around supplies that came in on the railroad and were stacked near the depot, to be used for putting in the pavement around Williamsburg. So Mr. Bean and Mr. Nelson saw each other frequently and came to know each other quite well. The two men used to go hunting together, and they played poker with some of the same friends.

That's why it was Jess's father to whom Charley reported that sometimes when the family went to bed, something would scratch on the outside of their boxcar home and keep them awake. With no trees around their home, they knew it wasn't branches. And sometimes, he said, whatever it was would knock on the outside walls.

The depot and the boxcar had been painted a dull gray. When the men went to examine the boxcar to look for the results of the scratchings, they saw shiny, swirly circles on the exterior walls, something like the swirls in fancy penmanship. But when they checked the mud after a rain, or the fresh snow in winter, there never were any strange tracks in it. So it seemed to Charley that they must have a ghost that liked to haunt them.

Charley said, "At first the ghost only showed up at night when we didn't have any lights on. When we did have light, it came from our kerosene lamp. It wasn't long before the ghost got braver and started to show up when the lamp was lit too."

Jess said later on, "My dad tried to help Charley get rid of whatever it was that was bothering them. One night, Dad carried a revolver and asked Charley and his family if it would be all right if he shot right through the wall if the scratching persisted."

Jess explained, "Dad figured if it was anyone else trying to give them a fright or just pester them or watch them, a shot would scare him away.

"Dad was inside with his gun. He and the Nelsons were all listening. Dad hoped to aim at a spot near where the scratching sounds were made. When the scratching started again, Dad alerted the Nelsons that he was going to shoot. He did, and the noises stopped. When the men went out there, they didn't see anyone or anything suspect. But the sounds started up again half an hour later, so the men didn't think it was anyone that lived around there and was just playing around. No sane man would return after being shot at."

Charley's ghost acquired a name all its own too. Jess told the story of how that happened.

"One night Gordon, who was interested in Model T Fords, was listening to the scratching on the wall. At that time the family didn't know that the ghost could think, but Gordon got the idea to give it sort of a test. He said, 'Make like a Model T going uphill.'

"Charley's ghost started rapping kind of slow," Jess said. "Then it slowed down some more, and just as if the Model T had reached the top of a hill and started down the other side, it gradually increased the tempo. By that, Gordon knew it could think or had some form or measure of intelligence. Then he asked it if it could understand two knocks for YES and three knocks for NO. Right away, it knocked twice to signify that it understood. That's how it came about that we could 'talk' to it," Jess finished.

After that, at any chance the boys had, when they heard the scratchings or the rappings, they tried talking to it. One of the first questions they asked was, "Are you dead?"

Immediately came two knocks for YES.

In answer to, "Were you a carpenter in your real life?" the boys heard three knocks for NO.

Another question was, "Are you a Protestant?" The answer came as three knocks.

"Are you a Lutheran?" Three knocks. NO. "Are you a Catholic?" YES.

They figured by answers to other questions that it was the ghost of a dead Irish peddler. That's why they started calling him "Irish."

Other people "talked" to Irish too. Mostly they were friends of the Nelson family or people that Jess and his father knew. They heard the answers: the two knocks for YES and the three for NO. And if the question required an answer in small numbers, one knock meant one year or one month or day, or one item, etc.

Anyone who came into the home could ask questions. Jess said, "When my brother was only five, someone told him to ask Irish a question. William, my brother, asked, 'How many fish are there in Old Man's Creek?' Irish couldn't answer a question like that with his YES or NO answers, so he just made a series of quick rappings. Maybe that meant 'Many fish.' We weren't sure."

Jess said, "Some other people who heard Irish were the mayor of Williamsburg, the newspaper editor, the priest, my own father and mother, and my uncle."

Then Jess continued, "This all happened over 70 years ago, right here in Williamsburg. There was another house in Iowa County too. It was the second place the Nelsons lived, also in Williamsburg. It was just half a block off of the square. It's gone now. But the rappings on the outside walls were heard there. I myself heard them quite a few times at both places."

People would sit on the high school lawn across from that house on warm summer nights just to listen. They could hear Charley's voice when he was asking Irish questions, and they could hear Irish's knocks in answer.

There were other questions Irish could answer. For example, he could tell whether one of the poker players had a good hand, or which prizefighter was favored to win the next fight. You could usually bank on his having the right answers, and some of the poker players got disgusted and quit playing when Irish ruined their game.

Apparently a dead Irish peddler had been buried at the site where the boxcar living quarters were set down along the Chicago, Milwaukee, and St. Paul railroad yard. Gordon and Jess checked out the crawl space under the boxcar once, but they couldn't find any bones or any other indication of a burial there. But maybe they didn't go deep enough.

Jess went on with his story. "My father and my Uncle Wallace even contacted a ghostbuster out of New York City. The locals had put together a pot of money. It totaled $5,000. Needless to say, the man went through the attic at the second place and mumbled something about radios and ventriloquism, but he couldn't explain anything clearly. He went back to New York City at his own expense."

Charley could get free passes for himself and his family because he worked for the railroad. When his mother-in-law died in another state, though, Charley wouldn't let his wife take the free pass and go down South to bury her. After that, Irish claimed to be the ghost of the mother-in-law, maybe giving Charley a hard time for not letting his wife go down to her own mother's funeral.

Later on, Mrs. Nelson passed away in their second home in town. Jess said that the daughter, Mary, moved away and married, and the son, Gordon, lives in another state. He said that Charley left town too.

Jess wrapped his story up with this emphasis: "I don't want the story of Charley's ghost to die with me. All of this really happened. It's not just a figment of my imagination."

A City of Many Ghosts

Evidently, Davenport would be a good place to live if you were interested in hosting ghosts. Or if you were a ghost, you could probably join a whole company of them there.

Jim Arpy, writing for the *Times-Democrat*, Davenport, wrote several stories about hauntings at the old Pi Kappa Chi fraternity house on Main Street in that city. Residents of the house at the time were students at the Palmer College of Chiropractic. Arpy related some very scary incidents that took place there, including heavy footsteps being heard, locked doors opening and closing, typewriter keys striking, and toilets flushing without human aid.

Arpy's May 11, 1972, story gave an account of celebrated Chicago medium Mrs. Irene Hughes' visit to the fraternity house. Hughes felt that the main spirit was that of a medical doctor who was also involved in politics. Later research revealed that a medical doctor had owned the home for a long time and had also been involved in politics. Hughes described the doctor/spirit as one who felt that he was right in most things and wanted the present occupants of the house to do things his way.

A few years later, Arpy wrote about another apparently haunted house in northwest Davenport. In this case, an adult couple were experiencing unexplainable incidents that left them frightened and puzzled. Both had been in good health when they began to remodel the old schoolhouse that became their new home; after that, both had been sick much of the time. The couple told of furniture sliding all the way across rooms, day and night. Lights and faucets mysteriously came on, seemingly by themselves; their TV and radio came on, and in general things happened that they didn't direct or initiate.

A daughter-in-law who spent some time visiting the same couple in that house fell several times as the result of what she described as a push. Dark figures were seen, loud knocks and heavy footsteps were heard, and other unexplainable things happened. Was the remodeled old schoolhouse haunted by teachers and students of earlier years? Do they return to rearrange the furnishings and set the house in order, according to their accustomed plan?

In an October 31, 1971, *Times* story, Arpy told about another haunted house in McClellan Heights. There, the children in one particular bedroom cried at night. When the parents went to check, they were always surrounded by a terribly cold area just outside that door—like a very cold, chilling wind they couldn't account for. When he researched, the owner found out that his house was built on land that was once part of old Camp McClellan, a Civil War training camp, and that his house was built near and possibly partly over a Native American burial ground.

A few days later, two staff writers wrote for Davenport's *The Leader* about a Davenport businesswoman who shared a house on Main Street with her elderly parents and "a friendly spirit named Elsie." That extra "presence" was felt both inside the house and out in the yard, where the businesswoman removed a lot of trees and shrubs and put in a new fence. A neighbor told the young woman that Elsie had once lived in the old house, loved it, and "spent long hours in the yard." It would seem that her presence was still being felt.

Arpy wrote of another huge old house in Davenport, this one on Ripley Street, where many young men had lived as students. The date and name of the newspaper were lost in the process of getting copies from the "Haunted House" file in the Davenport Public Library's Special Collections Room. But the article made it clear that the roomers in that house had been very frightened a number of times by various phenomena, including a man's figure, a strange cat, heavy footsteps, a cold room where a presence was felt, and locked doors being found unlocked.

In *The Leader* of October 29, 1986, the McClellan Heights house was again featured by staff writer Rita Pearson. Another story by Michael Ashcraft featured a young couple and their first house, an old one. When they first went through it, it felt "old and sad and lonely." The couple wanted to restore an old house; "they wanted one with spirit." The one they got had windows that came open by themselves even if they were nailed shut. Apparently, it had spirit enough for them. What kind of spirit is lost in the file at the Davenport library, as page C2 of that newspaper is missing? Perhaps the spirit itself purposely misplaced the rest of the story.

Do Playmates Live Upstairs?

When Jim and Judy first moved into their house in a quiet neighborhood in southwest Cedar Rapids, they didn't know it was still occupied. True, the people who sold them the house had moved out, but they hadn't told the buyers about any invisible occupants.

One evening about a year later, Judy and her 4-year-old, son Colin, were visiting Judy's mother. That left Jim at home with their infant son, Hunter. While Hunter slept, Jim was reading—until such a loud noise shook the house that Jim was nearly scared out of his chair in the den. The den and the garage shared a wall, which made Jim think someone had rammed a car into the side of the garage.

He didn't see anything wrong out there when he looked out the windows. He couldn't leave Hunter there alone, and he did not want to disturb his sleep, so he called 911. When the police came by, they looked around but couldn't find anything that would point to a crash. Jim said, "In fact, they looked at me as if they thought I had been drinking. Then, as time passed, I sort of forgot about the experience."

One evening several months later, Jim got out of his chair in the den to go out to the kitchen. He explained, "The den is sunken, with two steps down into it from a small landing." Then he went on to tell what happened. "As I neared the landing, I had the sensation that a medium-size dog had just jumped into my arms. But we don't have a dog and none appeared. Even though I had seen nothing, I had a strong mental image of the dog. It had been there, somehow. Judy saw me as I jumped back in shock, and she asked, 'Did the dog jump up on you just now?' That was when I learned that Judy had had the very same experience in the same spot in that house."

The dog incident made them think back to when they first moved in. They started wondering if the sellers were so anxious to bargain with them because of spooky experiences they had had. They had left a lot of things in the house, including an upstairs bed, fully made. Jim and Judy thought that was really unusual, especially now that strange things were happening to them. And the sellers had also sold their business and left town and had not come back since.

Jim remembered, too, that when his sister stopped by with a housewarming gift, he had noticed her reaction. He knew about her previous experiences with ghosts and poltergeists. He remembered that she moved quickly but thoughtfully through the house, pausing here and there, as if aware of a presence, but said nothing to them as to having sensed anything.

After the dog experience, things were pretty quiet until the 1992 Christmas holiday season. From then on, Jim said, "Our comfortable lifestyle in the home of our dreams changed dramatically."

Jim's niece Janelle and her boyfriend were with them a few nights after Christmas. Jim, Judy, Colin, Hunter, Janelle, and her guest were all in the den watching movies when Jim and Janelle heard the door to the upstairs stairway open and close. Though the door was in a different part of the house, they recognized its distinctive sound. Realizing that all the people in the house were right there in the den, the adults investigated, only to find the door "solidly shut," as Jim put it.

More experiences started to surface. Janelle stopped by the next night to tell about what had happened to her the summer before, while she was housesitting for them. That same door had actually opened and closed one night while she was there alone. Though she had had some "bad vibes," as she put it, before that, she had said nothing. Jim said, "Janelle was a very independent, confident 21-year-old used to living alone in her apartment. She wasn't easily frightened, but she was that weekend here, alone. She ended up sleeping on the couch, while the door opened and closed on its own several times that night. She tried to blame it on a draft."

After the December repetition of her experience, it seemed that it occurred whenever Janelle came by. Jim said, "We consulted experts. They suggested, one, that it could be the ghost of a boy who might be 'flirting' with Janelle, or two, that Janelle and I together create some type of energy that triggers supernatural happenings in the house."

On New Year's Eve, Janelle and her girlfriend Bobbi stopped by to celebrate. That night, after the boys were asleep in bed, the adults were watching rented movies and playing some games when suddenly they all looked at each other as they realized there was someone else in the den with them—a presence or a spirit that they each knew was there, though they actually saw nothing physical.

As Jim made an attempt to describe it, he said, "The presence moved in a half-moon configuration from one doorway to the other, and a cold draft absolutely filled the room. We sat tight in our chairs, but I finally got up enough nerve to leave my chair and describe my sensation to the others. They all felt the same type of movement, as though all of us sensed exactly the same thing, but none of us saw anything real that could be described easily.

"We moved from the den into the front living room in the other part of the house. At that point we all became extremely frightened. Janelle described the spirit as actually standing over her, touching her. Yet no one saw anything! She sat and sobbed for the rest of the evening, and we all stayed up until nearly 4 a.m., scared to pieces! When midnight came, we didn't even think about wishing each other a happy new year!

"We think the spirit 'lives' in our upstairs and that there is also a presence in our basement. My sister thinks so too."

Jim said that he and Judy were both puzzled. In fact, they were frightened enough that each of them started waiting outside for the other after work, until they could both go in together. They even adjusted their work schedules so they could leave at the same time each morning.

They were both truly afraid, even though they didn't feel that the presence or presences represented evil or the Devil at all. It was just so strange. They wished the contacts with the spirit or spirits would end. At night, they closed their bedroom door and pulled the covers up to their chins, yet were afraid and were unable to sleep. Some nights they barely slept at all, meanwhile trying not to say anything that would scare the boys.

But they soon learned that Hunter had already known something was different there. When he was 3, he burst into their bedroom one Saturday morning with a very strange look on his face. "He truly looked possessed," Jim said. "We followed him out to the living room. Hunter was frantic. While he tried to open the upstairs door so he could go up there, he was all the while yelling, 'Kids, come back! Kids, come back!'

"Hunter appeared to be sleepwalking. When we got him fully awake and talked about it later, he told us that three boys, all older than he was, 'lived' in our upstairs. He thought they were maybe about 6, 8, and 12. Hunter said that at night they would all come down to the boys' room. They wanted to play with their toys. Sometimes they were hungry too. He said they would all sleep in our upstairs in our king-size bed sometimes, and they came from the house next door through our attic, into our upstairs, and down into his and Colin's room.

"We know all about young children having very active imaginations, and we know sometimes children have imagined playmates they talk to, but this was something different. We saw it in Hunter's face as he tried to open that door and get the kids to come back. It seemed so real to us that we checked into who actually lives next door, but there were no children living there at this time.

"After learning about Hunter's experiences, we feel certain that the spirits living in our home are the spirits of children. Hunter also says that sometimes at night their Daddy drives them to our house to drop them off to play. Sometimes he even stands in the doorway to our boys' room and watches them play. That made us wonder if the garage/car crash sound was related. But how could it be?

"We contacted two professional exorcists," Jim said. "One of them suggested lighting white or light-colored candles and doing prayer rituals. We did that as a group of three adults—the two of us and Janelle. The other exorcist suggested hanging pictures of Jesus Christ throughout our home to protect us from potential evil. We tried that, too, although no one believes our entity to be evil. We feel that our ghost or ghosts are friendly, and since the 'weird' things tend to happen at holiday time, we believe positive experiences such as a holiday trigger their behavior."

Jim and Judy finally contacted some of the former owners of the home to ask if they had had any experiences like theirs. The family they had bought the house from were evasive, but they did admit to finding the house "full of religious paraphernalia." They said they removed all of it and burned it. The man said that a few things had been left in the attic, but he had been afraid to go up there to get them, "so maybe they're still there."

The man's wife said the only thing she ever felt weird about was the trim along the entire length of the front of the house. The trim was made up of unusual shapes—stars and circles carved into a decorative strip, and painted the same as the house. Jim and Judy had noticed it, but hadn't paid much attention to it.

The former housewife also told them that one time a stranger stopped by, rang the doorbell, and told them they should get out of the house because of those shapes, "those evil signs." But then, she also said she didn't believe the person enough to act on the warning.

Before that couple lived there, the occupants were grandparents of some of Jim and Judy's coworkers. They checked to find out if there were any weird incidents then, but only found out that the home was always filled with love and that holidays were a special time. Yet, they learned that each of those two elderly occupants had died at separate times in that same house, in the room where Hunter claims to host visitors and in the bed where the two boys sleep.

"We don't exactly know where to go from here," Jim said. "We love our home, but we don't feel totally comfortable with what's happening. Sometimes we feel perfectly safe. Then something else happens, and we're unsure.

"During the most trying weeks when we were almost afraid even to come home at night, Judy and I finally got out one day just for a chance to relax for a few hours' drive. The boys were with Janelle at her apartment. We had stayed home so much, just to avoid the fear upon returning, that it felt really good to get away and relax once.

"When Judy and I went back home, Janelle hadn't brought the boys back yet. We sat down in the den, still feeling more comfortable and relaxed than we had for a long time, when a huge moan came from the corner of the den. Someone or something moaned once, then again about 10 seconds later. I was more scared than ever before. I thought I'd have a heart attack and die right then and there. If I hadn't been barefoot, I believe I would have run out the door and abandoned the place. But there was deep snow outside. We tried to convince ourselves that the noise had come through the flue of the fireplace, or from an electronic toy, but we knew it didn't. We both heard it, experienced it.

"That same week, we were called to a friend's house on an emergency. Janelle and her boyfriend came to babysit the boys. When Judy and I returned, the young couple were huddled together in absolute terror in a corner of the kitchen. What had frightened them so? They told us that while they were in the den, the electronics in the house—the VCR, stereo, lights, everything—had gone bonkers, all these things turning themselves on and off. The two couldn't abandon the children (they were in bed), so they waited in absolute fear for us to come back. Janelle's boyfriend never did come back to our house.

"I can't blame him a bit. Even though we think of our ghosts, or whatever they are, as friendly spirits, I'm home alone as I write this down for you—and it's giving me the goose bumps even as I write."

Fredrica May Have Moved to Fisher

Numerous references in Iowa State University publications and in Ames city newspapers easily lead one to believe that there was, or perhaps is, indeed a ghost in the school's theater buildings. In fact, it seems that the ghost, formerly occupying Shattuck Theater, moved on to the new Fisher Theater, once Shattuck was demolished.

Shattuck was originally built on the Ames campus in 1900 as a stock-judging pavilion (sometimes sheep, sometimes horses). It was a gray, round, frame structure located near the Landscape Architecture and Journalism buildings. In 1931, when it was redone, it became the home of the Iowa State Players and was used as a theater workshop until 1973 when Fisher Theater was ready for use.

Iowa State Players had been established by Fredrica V. Shattuck shortly after she came to ISU in 1914 as the first director of theater on campus. At first, the building was called the theater workshop. Articles state that it was not easy to establish dramatics in the technical school, but Fredrica was interested, and she worked enthusiastically to do that.

In 1960, the building was renamed Shattuck Theater in her honor. She had retired in 1948, and she died in 1969. That's when folks who have been on the campus and in theater say strange things began to occur there.

Professors who had directed plays and students who performed in them or helped with sets, lighting, etc., were not happy to hear that Shattuck would be torn down, but it was deteriorating and restoration would be too costly. Perhaps they were not the only ones who would miss it. It seems that, although the students could work there on productions with very little supervision, they hesitated to be there alone, especially at night. They thought it had a ghost.

Perhaps it did. Perhaps it was the ghost of Fredrica Shattuck. Articles from the Special Collections/Archives of the Iowa State University Library relate numerous instances of encounters with a ghost in the stock-judging-pavilion-turned-theater. One student reported outside doors opening on a snowy evening, when all doors were locked. Then came the sound of footsteps followed by a door closing. But there were no tracks out in the snow other than that student's own footprints from when he had entered.

Sherry Hoopes, a former ISU speech professor who had also directed several plays, took part with others in a seance in the theater. As they did, though nothing else noteworthy happened, the group all had the feeling that someone was watching them.

A group of students rehearsing late one night heard sounds above them, on the stage. When they went up to check, they saw a wheelchair move across the stage to the center and come to a halt, facing the audience, in monologue position. It was Fredrica's old wooden wheelchair. She had used it in her later years, after she had suffered a stroke, before her death. It had been kept as a prop after her death. But who had pushed it across the stage into that position? None of the students would admit to having done it as a joke. Besides, none of them were in the backstage area where it rolled from, when it came across the stage.

Others, including Burt Drexler, a former Iowa State speech professor, say that lights in the building go on and off without reason.

Some say that Shattuck's ghost moved to the new Fisher Theater in 1973 or 1974. They believe that because of some strange things that have happened there.

One actor heard his name screamed out during a rehearsal. No one there at the time would take the blame.

When Joseph Kowalski, an assistant professor of theater, was looking for the light switches in the dark upper backstage area, a voice suddenly said, "They're over by the door." When he found them and switched them on, no one was up there with him.

At another time, Kowalski was working alone in the costume shop when, according to Ken Uy's article in the *Ames Daily Times* of October 28, 1993, the items he was using, such as scissors and a tape measure, disappeared. After a while, they appeared again—not where he would have left them as he worked, but all gathered together in one spot.

Another time, music came over the loudspeakers when no one had started it. When Brooks Chelsvig, the sound technician, arrived, he and Joe Libby, former house manager, went upstairs to look into it. The music stopped. When they unlocked the sound booth, they found one of Chelsvig's tapes in the tape deck. It had been played halfway through. But no one else was there.

Kerry Bell, the co-house manager, and a friend went to Fisher the night before the opening night of *Rumors*. Kerry realized it was almost midnight, and her friend was dragging her feet about that, but they wanted to put up a display using the actors' photos. Riding the elevator back downstairs from the upper level, Kerry pushed the emergency stop button as a joke. She thought she might as well scare her friend a little. But as she switched it off again, it kept on going, and it kept going for about 10 minutes. When Kerry's friend screamed, the elevator moved back up to the second floor and the doors opened. Needless to say, both Kerry and her friend left the building at a fast run.

All of these incidents seem to support the claims that the Shattuck ghost had moved to Fisher.

According to an article by Vicki Shannon in the *Iowa State Daily* of October 30, 1978, Molly Herrington explained the ghost this way: "She's just letting us know that she's still around. She comes out to tell us she's glad we're still doing theater at ISU, since she's the one who started it all."

Shannon quoted Herrington: "At night, ghosts will come out and re-enact their 'big scene.' Sometimes they put together a whole show." Herrington had also told Shannon that old theater troupes always left a gas lamp burning in the middle of the stage to show ghosts their way.

The Ghost of
Brush Creek

In the late 1850s, a schoolhouse had been moved in to Brush Creek. But before the turn of the last century, the growth of the settlement necessitated a larger building. A brick, two-story, forty-by-sixty school was built in 1877.

In the 1890s, children of school age were used to walking to school, even for 3 or 4 miles from outlying homes. On their way to and from school, the Brush Creek children refused to walk past one particular farm. They would beg rides in the buggies or wagons of passing neighbors rather than walk anywhere near the dense woods surrounding that farm.

When the house and the big barn were built, they were set on the edge of the woods, just as many pioneers' homes were. Brush Creek, running nearby, should have been the place for children to go fishing, but they wouldn't go near it. Brush Creek Canyon provided an ideal place for the young people to search for yellow lady's slippers or jack-in-the-pulpits on lovely spring days, but they didn't.

When the parents heard their children talking about the farm, they asked questions. The children said that the woods were haunted. On being questioned further, the youngsters said they had seen someone moving in the brush between the huge oak trees back a few yards from the roadside fence. When they were asked if they had ever been approached by the person, they said, "No. Never. It's more like he wants to hide from us." Another said, "It's too scary. How do we know he won't bother us sometime?" "Besides," a third said, "my big sister Ella quit working there last month, and Ella knows three other hired girls that quit working for the old man before she did."

"He must be real mean, if no one will stay there to work for him. But how can that pretty girl that married him stay? How can Jennie stand it?"

One of the fathers said, "Maybe it isn't the old man that everyone's afraid of." But he didn't explain, and the children wondered what he meant.

Jennie had married the 75-year-old widower on June 6, 1883. She wept at her own wedding, people said. She hadn't wanted to marry the old man in the first place. Her parents had insisted. Many said that Jennie's parents were thinking of themselves and how they could benefit from his wealth.

Jennie was lovely and she was young. Everyone knew there was a young man her own age who loved her and wanted to marry her. Yet she was forced to marry the old man, so much older than she. He didn't even have children or grandchildren for her to learn to love. Jennie didn't care about the house or the money as much as she cared to be happy with someone who really loved her.

The Brush Creek settlement knew the young man who wanted to marry Jennie, but he disappeared shortly after her marriage. Some thought he had gone to another state to find work. Others guessed he'd met with an accident and been killed. There were plenty of rumors as to what had happened. The rumors surfaced again almost 20 years later when people started to wonder if the shadow in the grove was his ghost or if it was himself come back for real, to be near Jennie.

The hired girls who quit one by one told about something or someone, maybe a ghost, that they thought was hiding in the house. They heard noises at all hours of the night, but they never saw anyone else around except the old man and his young wife. Yet food disappeared regularly from the pantry. And in the back part of the house near the kitchen, the smell of decay came through the walls or floor. The girls were afraid their mistress would think they weren't keeping the kitchen tidy, and it worried them. For that reason and because they were honestly frightened, they left.

On the night of August 3, 1903, two people passing by the farm heard screams. They rushed to the house, where they found Jennie crying hysterically. In one corner of the bedroom they found the old man's corpse, his neck broken by hands that had to be stronger than his wife's.

In the investigation that followed, Jennie was questioned. When she was able to overcome her shock and fear, she said the man that killed her husband was a prowler who first strangled him and then raped her. She gave the impression that she didn't know him and had never seen him before.

Jennie kept to herself for about two years after she had been widowed. Eventually, when she began to go out again, some men in the church noticed she was still an attractive woman. One of the men began to court her and soon asked to marry her. She agreed, and they set a date for their wedding. One evening, he came to visit her. He was shocked to find Jennie's body in the bedroom. Her neck had been broken.

The sheriff of Fayette County was determined this time to find the murderer. He swore in three deputies and they searched the house thoroughly, spending seven hours combing every cranny from the attic to the crawl space under the floors.

There, in the crawl space, they found the remains of a man's body, dressed only in rags. With it they found evidence that he had lived there for many years. The body was identified as that of the young man who had disappeared some 20 years earlier. The sheriff and his men were puzzled. They had found the corpse and the garbage, but they still had a problem. Though this person could have murdered the old man two or three years earlier, how could he have killed Jennie, when he had evidently been dead for over a year? How could he have broken her neck?

Today the children still refuse to walk by the old farm. Though Brush Creek is now a part of Arlington, the farm is still there in the northwest part of town. Its buildings are falling apart and its woods have grown even more dense and frightening. The children and the young ladies are still afraid, though the old man and his unwilling bride are buried and the crawl space under the house is empty. Young lovers in Arlington today never stroll by those woods in the moonlight. They feel threatened, they say. They prefer to walk the other way, through another part of Arlington, as far from the woods and the farm as possible—even if their chosen path could take them through the very cemetery where the three people in the story were each in turn safely and permanently buried.

The details that make this story possible were apparently written up by a Rob Robbins for an area newspaper, in the late 1800s when the incidents took place.

The Ghostly
Bell Ringer

The limestone church with spires shooting up into the sky can be seen for a long ways in this northeast Iowa town on the Mississippi River. The bells still ring today, but this story took place over 80 years ago.

The bells were at the top of the tallest spire, and Janetta had to climb steep rock steps to even reach the ropes. Her father, dead four months now, had proudly done this special job for his church, as had his father before him. Since no sons remained, Janetta was to ring the bells this Sunday.

She had often come here with her father, going to the very top of the steeple, before the bells were rung. Janetta would then peek out at the winding Mississippi. Sometimes fancy steamboats would be going past, so elegant and rich, their paddlewheels slowly scooping water. Or she might see some of her father's friends, fishing for some of the huge river catfish to sell at the market.

She climbed the stairs slowly, wondering if she might see any fancy boats today. Leaning against the rough wall to catch her breath, she heard the bells begin to peal. She ran up the last short flight, jerked open the door, and screamed and screamed! The dark figure ringing the bells was her father. Dressed in his black funerary suit, he was rhythmically pulling the rope as he had many times before. He looked at and through her.

Still screaming, she ran down the steps. She did not stop running or screaming until she reached the old German priest's home. Janetta was so terrified and winded that she could only gasp, "Bells, church...my father." The old priest sent her into the house and went to the church immediately.

Janetta nervously stood by the window, not seeing the cool beauty of the fall day. The same river she had looked forward to examining went unnoticed, although bordered by banks of blazing reds and golds. She was still standing at the window, unseeing, when the priest returned. Turning, she pressed her back to the wall and gripped the limestone sill fiercely.

"Did you see...?"

"Janetta, sit down." He gestured toward a large overstuffed chair. "Your father, he is in purgatory and must have a mass said. He is in between—not Heaven, not Hell. We have a mass this morning at Kirche. He will rest then."

Mass was dedicated to Janetta's father that morning, for reasons only Janetta and the old priest knew. True to the priest's word, her father never reappeared, and Janetta continued to ring the bells for many years.

Gretta

There was nothing unusual about the architecture of the house in Calmar. It was an ordinary smaller home, built in the 1920s, with two rooms up and two down, a basement, and a garage.

What was strange about it was that things were happening there when no one was at home. No one that was supposed to be there, at least. Window shades would roll up and down in the daytime, as if someone followed the sun around to keep the house cool. Windows on the east side were opened in the forenoon, as if to let in fresh air. The neighbors said that by noon, they were always closed again. Yet the door was always locked, too, when Dex, the rightful tenant, came home from work.

Dex wondered about these strange goings-on. There were others too. Some mornings when he woke up, a woman would be hovering over the bed, looking down at him. When she appeared, she was dressed in black and wore a wide-brimmed black hat decorated with pink roses and a pink ribbon. The roses were like the ones on the sturdy old bush in the backyard. A neighbor told Dex they were Tiffany roses.

Dex began to wonder if the woman who had lived in the house many years before was showing her displeasure over being placed in a care center against her will. In life, she had always been especially tidy about herself and her home and yard. She had tended the roses herself as if they were her children. Maybe she had come back now to set things straight.

Dex, the paying tenant, slept in a waterbed he had bought before baffles were built into them. Used to its normal movement, he easily recognized when someone standing at the side of the bed pushed down on the mattress, making a wave that moved him up and down, up and down. He got up once to turn on the light and look around, but no one was there. It kept on happening. It grew worse, the bed's movements stronger.

"The pushing presence made me feel smothered," Dex said. "I felt bound by a force that kept me from moving. Once, the bed lifted up with me in it. All of a sudden, I was looking down at the top of the dresser. I could see every item on that dresser. Not in a mirror. It didn't have a mirror. I could even see what time it was on my pocket watch lying there. It was just past midnight."

Eventually, Dex got disgusted with the situation, the unsettling incidents, and the lack of sleep. "I decided to try coming to terms with Gretta, my nickname for her. I said out loud, 'Now, look here, lady. I'm gonna live here. I'm not moving. If you're gonna live here, too, let's come to some kind of agreement. You come and go as you want, but leave me alone. I live here, too, you know, and I intend to stay and to get a good night's sleep every night.'"

His sudden tirade seemed to tone down Gretta's spirit a bit. The bed still moved some, but not as much. The radio started popping on spontaneously, and gentle footsteps could be heard on the stairs to the second floor. Scratching sounds as of branches moving across upstairs windows were frequent, but there were no trees or windows outside the upper level of the house.

With its simple peaked roof coming right down to the side walls, only the end walls and the dividing wall upstairs boasted much wall space. One day, Dex noticed that the inner wall had developed a brownish stain. He checked, but found no roof leak, nothing that would explain such a spot. Besides, the stain didn't start at the ceiling. It showed up in the lower part of the wall. Dex painted over it. Before long, the stain showed through again. He learned to keep the paint and brush handy. He painted that one bedroom wall seven times, but the ugly brown kept coming through, and it certainly defied explanation.

Dex's wife added to his story. She said that once, before they were married, she was in the house alone. "I had the tape player going," she said. "The tape I was playing had one song about ghosts. When the tape reached that song, it went wild, jumbling the music terribly, like a frenzied person trying to sing. But the rest of the songs had come through just fine."

She added that Gretta's house had push-button light switches—not turndogs, not up-and-down flips, not sideways flip buttons, but round buttons you poked in while the other one above or below it popped out. They clicked when you turned the lights on or off using them. "I could hear one light switch upstairs clicking on and off that same day. I just got out of there in a hurry. I wasn't about to go upstairs alone and check it out."

Dex said, "That was the last strange happening in the house in Calmar. Later, I did move out."

Do ghosts haunt the places they have lived, or do they follow the people they have haunted? This couple hopes the latter is not true. They feel they have had their fill of ghostly presences and forces. They say that so far, in their present home, there have been no problems.

Hollow Haunts

There are several stories about frightening experiences taking place in one of the hollows in Allamakee County. Because of the topography of northeast Iowa, there are many ravines or hollows with creeks or rivers such as the Turkey River, the Yellow River, the Volga, or the Upper Iowa. The deep ravines are the result of water running down and through them for so long that it has worn the limestone away.

The depressions, called hollows, are usually surrounded on three sides by slopes or limestone bluffs varying in height and overgrown with trees and brush. Caves, once accessible, are hidden by vegetation or have disappeared when their roofs caved in. Because of the numerous creeks and rivers, there are bridges, some in good repair and some closed because they are no longer safe or they lead to nowhere.

One such bridge is a one-lane span with a dead end beyond it. In fact, vehicles crossing it can only go far enough to park in the grassy area at the other end of the bridge. There is no room to turn around. The terrain is rough with rocks, and it slopes sharply upward. The grass is tall and helps to make it an ideal location for wildlife; it is also fairly quiet, day and night. Bobcats have been seen and heard around the bridge. There is no through traffic, therefore little danger to animals crossing the road.

About 60 years ago, some people lived in a long, narrow shack resembling a railroad car set on a side slope near the bridge. About 50 years ago, the farmer who owned the land built a couple of log cabins and a shed. They are gone now, though they still appear in many stories.

Perhaps because of its secluded location, strange events have taken place in the hollow marked by the dead-end bridge. The stories told about the hollow sparked curiosity and brought on many hunts for the spook or the bigfoot or whatever was in the hollow.

One of the hunts took place on a fall night, when a group of Decorah High School students piled into two cars and headed east on Highway 9. They were as curious as anyone, and they were determined to find out if what they had heard was true.

After leaving the highway, they traveled downhill on an unmarked road. On one of the many turns, three raccoons scampered off the shoulder of the road. Only a few distant farm lights glimmered through the trees before even they were cut off by the bluffs on that quiet, overcast night. No stars or moon brightened their view—only their own headlights as one car followed the other around curve after curve.

The students had been told by their friends that the way to set the mood was to tell scary stories along the way. That was what they did. The stories raised questions in their minds. Was there really a bigfoot in northeast Iowa? Did an eccentric hermit live in those hills? Had someone actually seen tracks and other signs left by a mutated human? Was the notorious wheat-colored creature a pony, or was it a strange monster? Was it the buckskin horse one farmer had reported?

The two cars finally rounded the last curve. The approach to the bridge and the shoulders of the road were soft from heavy autumn rains. With the river below and the still, humid air all around, the ground would dry slowly in the gully. Arriving first, the Camaro crossed the bridge and parked in the grassy area just beyond. It would have to back across the bridge to get onto the road again. The Firebird followed, but instead of crossing the bridge, it backed off into a muddy place.

Pete Brandt saw that he had gone too far and had one wheel stuck in the mud so he and his passengers worked on getting the Firebird unstuck. He tried gunning the engine, and some passengers tried pushing to inch the car back and forth, shouting instructions to the others trying to get in or out of the car or the mud. In the general clamor and confusion, none of them paid attention to what their friends who had arrived in the other car were doing.

Meanwhile, Steve Bryant had talked his carload into getting out of his Camaro. They stood in the grass close to the car and looked around and listened, hoping to settle the big question once and for all. They only heard the river flowing over rocks.

Sherri Jacobs and Tina Miller moved out a few yards toward the nearest bluff. Just ahead, something floated through the brush against the wall of rock. They heard the rustling of wet leaves and grass and the cracking of twigs. A shadowy, wheat-colored figure floated through the bushes and disappeared into a dark spot beyond the old, broken-down cabins. In a lull in the noises from their friends, others near the Camaro heard a loud bawling, bleating sound. Or was it a terrible, screaming cry? With the engine of the Firebird still running and the noise of the river, it was hard to tell. Besides, it echoed. No one waited to find out what it was. Screaming, the students piled into the Camaro in just seconds, and Steve began to back his car onto the bridge. But the other car still blocked its access to the road.

Hearing screaming and car doors slamming, the others knew something had scared their friends. Six of them promptly lifted the Firebird and its driver out of the mud and onto the firm stretch of road even as they jumped in. They headed away from the bridge, back toward the friendly raccoons and the solid, logical highway before the other car reached the road. Then the Camaro backed off the bridge so fast that it, too, was on the way back to town within seconds.

But that wasn't the end of it. They told their friends, of course, and another attempt to solve the mystery of the spook took place a few nights later when three fellows decided to go out there. They planned to go by daylight. They left Decorah after school, but by the time they rounded all the curves and arrived at the old bridge, it was dusk after all. They drove onto the bridge, knowing they would have to back off later. They sat in their car, listening through open windows. When they heard a long, bellowing sound, they dared each other to get out and look into the riverbed below. With the flashlight, they saw a fuzzy, furry thing with a shaggy, flowing mane. It scared them into a mad scramble back into their car. Something below the bridge knocked hard against the metal supports, vibrating the whole bridge and their car with it.

When they backed off and turned the headlights on, they saw something disappearing into a cave-like opening in the bluff, behind a broken-down shack. Feeling relatively safe then, the three decided to get out again and shine their flashlights down into the riverbed. There in the thick mud around the bridge supports, they could just make out the outlines of deep tracks that resembled the shape of a human foot, but were three times as big. The boys left quickly.

Others have tried to look farther into the area of the cave, hoping to find its opening and the creature that supposedly lives in it. They have never gotten closer than a couple hundred feet before they, too, have been frightened away by a low, bawling sound or a shrill, screaming, catlike cry or a shadowy movement against the bluff.

The old buildings deteriorated and were burned down with the landowner's consent. The bridge was closed due to the weakening of the approach. Only the mystery of the haunt of the hollow remains.

"Is That You, Fred?"

Matt's family had moved to town late in 1991. Matt and Kimberly became schoolmates and their families were soon friends. One night, both families were seated around the table in Matt's home in their town in Cedar County. The hour was late, but they were involved in their game of Trivial Pursuit and weren't ready to give it up.

Suddenly everyone heard the front door open. They weren't expecting anyone at that time of night. Knowing that the house used to be a funeral home, they all thought of the possibility of ghosts. Someone made a comment like, "I wonder whose ghost is coming back to finish the game with us." Everyone laughed about that. Then one of the group asked, "Is that you, Fred?" At that, the door swung shut again.

One of the players said, somewhat sarcastically, "Gee, Fred, don't go away mad." The door opened again, about halfway, then slammed shut.

No one was laughing anymore. They all sat riveted in their chairs and looked wide-eyed at each other and at the door.

The game was forgotten while Inis, Kimberly's mother, asked Matt's mother, "Is this the first time anything like this has happened?"

Sherri said, "I have no idea what went on here before we moved in. But there have been some weird things going on since we came."

Inis asked, "What kinds of things? People you can't see walking in and out and slamming the door, like tonight?"

"No, not that," Sherri answered. "But we have heard footsteps in the upstairs when no one is up there. Sometimes it's in the daytime, sometimes at night."

By then the children were getting curious about what they were hearing from their mothers. Matt said, "Tell them about the chair, Mom."

Sherri told about the old rocking chair in the attic. She said, "Sometimes when we go up there, we find it rocking all by itself."

Matt and Kimberly wanted to go up to the attic right away to see if it was rocking right then, but Inis thought they should wait until another time. She picked up her things as she said, "Come on, kids. It's time we went home. There is school tomorrow, you know. And besides, I don't want you having nightmares about ghosts."

From that night on, both families referred to the mysterious, unseen caller as "Fred, the ghost that lives upstairs," and Kimberly's family would add, "in Matt's house."

On another night a couple of weeks later, Kimberly and Matt did go upstairs in Matt's house.

The chair wasn't rocking when they got up there, but that wasn't their main objective anyway. They wanted to see if they could contact Fred. They knew how to use a Ouija board, and they hoped they could get Fred to talk to them.

It took a while, but finally on the first contact, Fred asked for a glass of water. The kids went down to the kitchen and filled a tall glass with ice cubes and water from the tap. Back upstairs, they set it on the card table and watched it, but Fred didn't drink it.

Matt and Kimberly went downstairs for a while. When they came back up, the glass was still full. They sat back down at the Ouija board. Matt asked, "Fred, if we count to three, will you drink the water we brought you?"

The pointer moved toward the "Yes."

Matt and Kimberly started counting. "One... two..." and before the count of three, the ice rolled around in the glass. The kids couldn't understand how it could move because there were so many ice cubes that they pushed against each other and the glass. Unless—was it Fred?

They both screamed and ran downstairs. But when they came up again, some of the water was gone. They felt that they really were in contact with Fred, and they asked him more questions.

"Fred, tell us how you died. Was it a car accident?"
The pointer moved over to the "No."
"Were you sick?"
"No."
"Did you die in a plane crash?"
"Yes."

"Can you communicate with animals, Fred? If you can, make Matt's hamster run his wheel."

The two watched the cage closely, and before a minute had passed, Hampi was running his wheel.

More screams, and another race down the stairs.

When they got their nerve up to go back upstairs, Matt and Kimberly noticed right away that the glass was in a different place.

"Now, how did that get moved?"

Kimberly answered, "I don't know for sure, but do you think Fred moved it?"

The two decided to stay up there and play Nintendo for a while and maybe keep their eye on that glass too. Matt wasn't having his usual success. Perhaps his mind wasn't on Nintendo. For whatever reason, he got mad and threw his controller on the floor. Hoping the set still worked, they both looked up and saw the image of a person, from the waist up, appear on the screen before it went dark.

When they ran downstairs again, they stayed there. They haven't tried to talk to Fred since, but they wish they knew more about him and his real-life experiences before he spent time in the funeral home and decided to haunt the upstairs in Matt's house.

The Jordan
House Spirit

West Des Moines, Iowa, is home to the Jordan House. The Jordan House was built in different phases between 1850 and 1870 by James Cunningham Jordan, an early pioneer. Jordan first raised cattle and then entered the fields of real estate and railroad development. He also served in the Iowa House of Representatives and Iowa State Senate. While in the legislature, Jordan promoted the change of the state capital from Iowa City to Des Moines. Despite his fame in these capacities, he would most likely have considered his role as a "chief conductor" on the Underground Railroad as his greatest accomplishment. Originally from Virginia, he detested slavery.

A dedicated abolitionist, Jordan helped many slaves on their quest for freedom. His house and farmstead were safe havens for escaped slaves on their journey.

Since punishment was severe for harboring runaway slaves, this was a dangerous occupation. John Brown and his party of 12 escaped slaves stayed at Jordan's farm in February of 1859 on their way from Kansas to the raid at Harper's Ferry. The Jordan House is one of several sites in the nation listed as an official stop on the Network for Freedom.

James Jordan and his wife, Melinda, were the first occupants in the house. After Melinda passed away, James married Cynthia Adams, and the couple eventually had 11 children. One of these children, Eda, is said to haunt the Jordan House.

The Civil War was making enemies of the North and South when Eda turned 3 years old. Eda was a lively, bright child, full of mischief. She might be found playing hide-and-seek in one of the rooms in the Victorian home or jumping out from behind a door to scare her sisters. One day she decided to slide down the walnut banister in the front hall. Since she knew this was forbidden, she waited until the hallway was empty. A small child, she struggled to get to the top of the banister, glancing around to make sure no one saw her. She finally managed to get on the banister and looked down. She hesitated—it seemed much farther now than when she was on the stairs. But being a bold child, she decided just to let go and slide down.

Her mother heard a crash and rushed to the front hall. Eda lay at the bottom of the stairs, ominously still. The doctor said she had broken her neck and there was nothing he could do. Eda died within a few days, having never regained consciousness. From that time on, family members would talk about Eda's spirit. If winter gloves were put down on a hallway table and later could not be found, they would say, "Eda's borrowed my gloves. Her hands must be cold." After electricity came, if the lights went out, they would say, "Eda doesn't like those lights. We'd better get out the candles she favors." If an event could not be explained rationally, Eda was the one responsible. They were not afraid of Eda's spirit; in fact, it provided them with some comfort to know she was still around. Perhaps Eda still stays in this house, loved as a child and accepted as a spirit in a home known for its hospitality and generosity to those in need.

Larsen's Poor Gertrude

Larsen Hall, built in 1907, is one of the oldest buildings at Luther College in Decorah. Only Sunnyside, Campus House, and Sperati House are older. Larsen was strictly a men's dormitory for at least 30 years before coeducation arrived at Luther.

Those are duly recorded facts of history, hardly ripe material for a ghost story, except for the attraction that old buildings have for ghosts. And there seems to be a ghost in Larsen Hall. She is called Gertrude. No one knows for sure when Gertrude first took up residence in Larsen, but she has been there for many years. Understanding her presence in a men's dorm in its early years depends on what facet of her spirit one accepts. But no matter which Gertrude prevails, her activity is limited to the third floor, in the north end of the east wing and in "short corridor." That's what students call the section between the east and west corridors, at the base of the U-shaped building. That part of the dorm provides rooms for regular students—men or women, as needed and designated, from fall to spring. In summer, a special program called Upward Bound occupies it for its six-week session. Those students have also learned to share their space with Gertrude.

Parts of the building not used for student rooms provide space for faculty offices and the college health service. Those who work there are sometimes startled by banging radiators or rattling windows on cold, windy days and nights. Those are normal sounds in an old building. Others are not. Babs Goswell, a retired health service director, remembers hearing office doors slamming in the building while she worked the night shift. A nurse, Marny Esbe, says she sometimes hears heels clicking down the hall very late at night, when the other offices are closed.

Most of the stories told about Gertrude happened in the last 20 years or so. Maybe the earlier stories have simply been forgotten. More recent Luther students and staff members, however, can easily recall at least one incident credited to Gertrude, even though they have never seen her. Gertrude has never been known to show herself to anyone. She does take the blame, though, for many acts, such as setting off the fire alarm once or twice a week in the middle of the night. An impartial person could almost feel sorry for Gertrude because she has been the scapegoat for a long time.

B.J. Jones tells about the hot, humid day in late June when she was especially tired after a heavy afternoon class schedule. She trudged wearily back to her room. All she wanted was to flop on her bed for an hour before she had to work a night shift at the Union.

B.J. pushed her door open and let her backpack slide to the floor. When she put her glasses on the dresser, she saw that its drawers were open and the closet door was closed—just the opposite of the way she left them at noon.

The next day, B.J. told her roommate, "I was just too tired to look in the closet. The last thing I thought of before I dropped off to sleep was that maybe Gertrude was in there. By the way, was she?"

Later that same week, Jake Fortney, the building custodian, found mud and sand on the floor of the shower in the basement bathroom. The window into the room from outside was also open. Jake had heard about Gertrude and he knew she lived up on the third floor, but he began to wonder if she had a friend on the outside who had visited his basement.

Another incident was told by Merilee Stovall and Jane Peoples, roommates their sophomore year. When they settled into Larsen on Labor Day weekend, Merilee chose the top bunk. "It's harder to make up," she admitted to Jane, "but I like the feeling of being on top of things when I get up."

"Not a bad idea for a college sophomore," Jane said.

The feeling didn't last long, though, for Merilee. She had to stand on a chair every morning to make her bed. Then she would do her hair and gather her books and papers for the day's classes, leaving her room tidy the way she liked it. She invariably found her bed unmade when she came back in the afternoon. The covers weren't just pulled back. The sheets were tied in fat knots and the blanket was rolled up kitty-cornered and draped over the end of the bed. Naturally, she felt a little perturbed about it and, eyeing Jane directly, asked more than once, "Gertrude again? Why does she always have to pick on me?"

One night Merilee had Jane's stereo on while she typed a term paper for religion class. Tired, and making too many mistakes, she turned the stereo off and went to bed early (early being maybe by midnight). She knew Jane wouldn't be back to their room until a local pub closed.

Merilee fell asleep easily, but was awakened not long after by strains of the song "All At Once" from the same album she'd been playing that evening. She hung over the side of her bunk to see if Jane was asleep. The security light in the parking lot shone in just enough for her to see that no one was in Jane's bunk. Merilee nearly exploded when she realized that Gertrude had visited again and that she would have to get up and turn the stereo off herself. "Everyone says, 'Poor Gertrude.' Why not, 'Poor Merilee?'" she grumbled.

Another time Gertrude visited the room occupied by Rick Workman and Joe Carter of the Upward Bound staff. They had stayed at the dorm over a Fourth of July weekend. The students and the rest of the staff were gone. Returning to the room alone late that sultry Saturday night, Rick sensed that someone was in the room. He knew it wasn't Joe. Joe had made a spur-of-the-moment decision to join a group on a canoeing and camping outing on the Upper Iowa. Rick had driven them and their canoes to Bluffton himself that morning. Rick was to meet him at the Knudson Canoe rental site across from Will Baker Park and bring him back to campus the next day.

Then who is in here? Rick wondered. He had checked the outside doors a half hour earlier to make sure no one had propped them open. That usually happened when the students were around, so he thought checking them once was enough for that night. He reached for the light switch. The bulb flashed and burned out just as it came on. He tried the fluorescent study lamp on the desk, but both coolwhite tubes were gone. Joe had the flashlight, so as a last resort, Rick lit a stub of a candle left from a murder game they had staged for entertainment the previous weekend. The flame flickered, then burned blue.

When he looked around, Rick saw all his clothes piled on the overstuffed chair near the desk. In the closet, at least a dozen hangers were neatly lined up in a row, with the hooks all hugging the rod in the same direction and each one hung with a long skirt, a dainty summer blouse, a knit shawl, or a braid-trimmed cloak. "And if she wore jeans," Rick muttered, "I'll bet I'd find them in my drawer!"

That night, a heavy downpour during a thunderstorm broke up the camping group just before dawn. When Joe, soaked and muddy and tired, came back up to the short corridor, he found Rick curled up sound asleep on the hall floor, still holding the key to their room in one hand and a stub of a candle in the other. The door was closed. In fact, it was locked. And when Joe tried to unlock it, his key refused to turn in the lock. "Gertrude!" he almost shouted.

Only two believable explanations have been offered for Gertrude. Each one attempts to make clear how she came to live in Larsen Hall and each leaves a little to the imagination. One story is that she was a brilliant 1918 Decorah High School graduate who dearly wanted a college education before Luther became coeducational. She was also needed at home to look after her mother, who had been widowed early in World War I and who suffered from a broken hip. Attending a local college was her only possible recourse. She was refused at Luther; the college wasn't ready for female students. Before the year came along when she could have been admitted, she was struck down while riding a bicycle on West Broadway. Her injuries were fatal. Those who believe in that view of Gertrude picture her as a sad but lovely young woman often wearing a long white dress with lace trim and carrying a white umbrella while she hung around for years, waiting to be admitted through the usual channels. She is still waiting. With so much time on her hands, she is likely to do her share of mischief.

The other more grim view is that Gertrude's lover was a senior who grew despondent over the second World War and his plight as a student. With grades so low that his graduation from Luther was seriously threatened, he supposedly hanged himself in 1945 in an old ice shed on the west side of Decorah. They say that when Gertrude heard what he had done, she dressed herself in a dismal charcoal-gray wrapper and a strikingly contrasting fancy bonnet and appeared at his funeral. Within a few months she, too, died of an unknown cause. Perhaps she willed herself to die. Later, as a ghost, she went up to his former room in the short corridor on the third floor of Larsen Hall to look for her lover. Her spirit felt most at home there and stayed from then on, to be as near as she could to his tragic spirit.

The Lost Books
of Moses

Some German immigrants believed faithfully that there were two lost books of Moses: the sixth and seventh books. Supposedly these books were used to cast spells on people. The spells could make your livestock sick, keep your cows from milking, prevent your butter from churning, or cause your crops to wither in the field. Often, German-language newspapers available in America would contain stories in serial form that featured the lost books.

One true story from Iowa centered around these books. A German man had come from the old country and settled in Clayton County in northern Iowa. He married a neighbor girl and they had three children. She died in childbirth and he remarried shortly. Five more children were born before the second wife died of influenza. Finally, the man married for a third time to

Helga, a vain young woman, who was not very popular with her stepchildren. The oldest daughter, Rosa, was nearly the same age as Helga. The new wife and her husband had two children, making a total of 10 children in the household.

After 10 years of marriage, the farmer died quite suddenly. Rosa, who had been close to her father, grieved greatly. Although her brother and sister had married and moved away, Rosa still lived at home. Housecleaning had always been Rosa's responsibility, as well as a number of outside chores.

Helga inherited everything. Her first step was to inform Rosa that she would have to move out. Relatives of the second wife were contacted to take the younger five stepchildren. The three oldest children were bitter, especially Rosa. Helga would not even let them take their mother's beautiful hand-worked tablecloth.

The widow and her two children now lived in style, as the old farmer had been frugal and hard-working. The farm was paid for, and there was gold and silver hidden in the old dry well.

Meanwhile, Rosa, who had moved in with her brother, went to her father's friends in an attempt to obtain a copy of the sixth and seventh books of Moses. Most talked about the books, but none could produce them. At last, she found the books with an elderly cousin. Rosa planned to curse Helga and her children by somehow invoking the books. But Rosa's brother, much as he hated Helga, would not allow a copy of the lost books in his house. Nor would her sister. So Rosa had another idea.

A clear summer day was fading into twilight. Helga was baking bread, humming a German tune when she heard thumping noises in the root cellar. Opening the trapdoor, she yelled down, "Stop making that noise, children! I must get this bread baked."

No one answered. Peering down into the dark, damp cellar she could see nothing, but the thumping noises got louder. Dropping the trapdoor, she went to get a candle. Just then her children came in. "Ma, who is that in the ditch?" they asked.

Looking out the front door to the road, Helga could just make out a small figure in a white dress walking up and down the ditch, carrying an open book. Helga felt a wave of panic. "Could you hear what she was saying?" she asked. They shrugged. "Funny words, they must be in her book."

Meanwhile the noises in the cellar were getting louder.

"Ma, what is that?"

"Nothing. Maybe a shelf has come loose. Go to bed."

After the children were upstairs, she yelled from the door, "Go away, you and your evil book!" The white figure never looked up and Helga, too, went upstairs to escape the walker and the noises in the root cellar.

The next evening it started over. After a week, Helga sent the frightened children to stay with her parents, but she refused to leave. The noises and the slender pale figure kept on, night after night, in rain and fog and wind. Although Helga told everyone in the area, no one but she and her children ever saw the apparition. Slowly, her corn crops started to turn from bright green to yellow. This the farmers could see. Much whispering was renewed about "those books."

Until now, Helga had been considered a desirable match for eligible farmers in the area. She was still young and pretty—and rich. Bachelors had started casually dropping by, discussing the weather or crops. Now that stopped. Despair took hold of Helga. Other than her father, she could not get anyone to come and help with chores or feed her hogs. Even her father was reluctant. He noticed the changes in the crops and noted that the hogs were lethargic, eating very little, and gaining no weight.

Helga's dream of herself as the rich wife of one of the handsome bachelors was disintegrating. She decided she would beg the white vision for mercy. From a safe distance, she threw herself on the ground and pleaded. The pale figure paused, hovered briefly, but then kept walking and chanting strange words Helga couldn't understand. Helga didn't get close enough to see the face of the apparition. Images were now created in her mind of a bleak and lonely future, an old, bent woman living in the poorhouse. Helga turned in desperation to the parish priest. He had offered his help earlier, but she had turned him down.

Helga's father and the parish priest met her at the farm in the daytime. The priest was shocked. Instead of the pretty widow who took pride in her looks, he saw a haggard woman with blue-black shadows under her eyes, wearing a filthy apron. Propped beside the door was an old shotgun.

"I cannot take this anymore! I will shoot her, and I will shoot whatever is making noises in the root cellar," she cried.

The parish priest examined the house and looked down into the gloomy darkness of the cellar. Then he walked out to the ditch, where the green grass grew thick and high, despite Helga's claim that something had walked here for a month or more. No other part of the farm had such lush, green grass. Thoughtfully, he went back in the house.

"Shall I shoot now?" Helga implored.

The priest shook his head. "You can shoot the thing in the ditch or you can shoot in the cellar. It will be the same."

Helga's father looked at him. "What do you mean?"

Patiently, the priest explained. "The figure in the ditch and the noises in the cellar are the same."

"How can one thing be in two places?"

"I do not know how. But it is."

Helga interrupted, "What can I do? I cannot live like this."

The priest was quiet for a long time. "You did a great wrong to your stepchildren. You must change that. I will talk to them. With their help I can remove this curse."

"But this farm is mine. It was left to me!" protested Helga.

"The curse is already at work," the priest reminded her. "Do you want the noises to continue? Do you want these evil spells on you and your children?"

"No, no," she cried. "Do what you must!"

The priest summoned Rosa to church, a place she had not been since her father died. No one knows what Rosa and the priest talked about, but people said Rosa came in with a bulky package and left empty-handed. The noises in the cellar stopped. The crops turned green again and the hogs grew. All the children from the first two marriages received an equal settlement.

Helga used her remaining gold to buy another farm on the other side of town. Rosa would take no gold, so Helga turned over the home farm to her. Rosa never married. Today the farm is owned by the descendants of her nieces and nephews. In a place of honor sits the old oak family table, covered with a fine, handmade tablecloth.

A Loud Knock

A retired teacher recalled an incident that took place over 60 years ago at a rural school in Allamakee County. She will be called Maria Thomasin in this story. Maria remembers the details well because she had come in the fall of 1922 to teach in the same school where another teacher who will be called Bertha Atkins had been murdered on December 21, 1921.

On that day two students had stayed after school to erase the blackboards and talk with their teacher, whom they adored. The girls were on their way home when they turned at the corner to see Bertha going down through the outside door to the basement to bank the fire for the night. It was getting dark, so they parted and walked to their respective homes.

The girls didn't know that a passing farmer had seen someone sitting on the hill behind the school that afternoon. He said later that he thought he recognized the man as one of the group that had stirred things up the previous year, when only cast members were allowed to come in to practice for a play that was to be a fundraiser. Those not allowed at practice had caused a disturbance, and some of them still held a grudge against the teacher for it.

Accounts of the incident indicate that the man seen on the hill on December 21 must have slipped down to the yard after school that day, after the last students left for home. He followed Bertha into the basement, where she would have been using the big, awkward scoop shovel to bank ashes over the live coals to hold fire in the stove for morning. She could have turned to see why the door had swung open again behind her. She may have recognized the intruder as one of the group who had been denied entrance the year before. At any rate, a member of his family said that he had come home late that day, but only long enough to change clothes and wash his hands before he left in a hurry. Only by bloodstains on the towel could they have surmised that he was concealing a wound on his hand. Perhaps Bertha, noting his angry expression as she turned around, had reached for the shovel again to defend herself. But he was apparently stronger, and in his burst of anger he was later reported to have beaten her on the head with a heavy piece of stovewood. Then he went out, locking the basement door as he left. After stopping at his own home, he stole a horse from the next farm and a saddle from another as he headed north into Minnesota. It wasn't until May of 1923 that the investigation ended.

The effects of the 1921 murder were long-lasting. When Maria arrived to teach the next fall, she could see that the children had heard details from their parents. She knew they were afraid because of what had happened.

Maria already had two years of teaching experience when she came to the school. She had developed a sense of responsibility and had confidence in her ability to handle her job. She and her new pupils had spent two months getting to know each other and had reached a level of mutual trust and acceptance. The lessons were going well. Maria was used to seeing that the pail was full of fresh water. She had caught on to coaxing the basement stove into heating the room above on these increasingly cold days.

On the afternoon of October 31, 1922, the pupils and their new teacher put their books up on the shelf and their papers and pencils into their desks before Halloween treats were passed out. Then they put on jackets and took popcorn balls and apples out into the crisp air for recess. They had no more than settled back into their desks and bent their heads over their books again before they all heard a loud knock on the door. Maria was at the front of the room, helping two young boys with their arithmetic. She asked Tony Baker, a seventh-grade boy sitting close to the door, to see who was there.

Tony opened the door. He said, "No one's here at all." Thinking about how loud the knock was and that evidently someone or something heavy had made the sound, Maria excused herself and went out with Tony to look again. Still no one; nothing. The snow shovel and mop hung on their hooks, and the broom hadn't tipped over in its corner. They looked outside, but saw no one. They looked in the outhouses, but all the students had come in after recess. A quick look into the basement gave no answer. By then, it was almost the end of the afternoon and the children were feeling a little shaken. The scary mood of the coming Halloween night was heightened by the unexplained sound.

The children thought about what had happened to Miss Atkins less than a year earlier. Maria tried her best to calm them before dismissal. She said, "It was probably just a dead branch that fell on the roof of the entry, and with the door shut we just didn't hear it right. You all have fun, tonight. And be careful."

Nevertheless, the younger ones all stayed close by the side of their older siblings and neighbors as they walked home that day. They talked about mysterious sounds, loud knocks, and ghosts. They couldn't forget about it. Fear had entered their hearts with that sudden, loud knock. Jeannie Marshall held onto Irene Godwin's hand while she asked, "Do you think it was Miss Atkins's ghost?" Elvin Young asked Jonathan King, "Do you know where the man is that killed that other teacher? Did they find him yet?" And Jonathan answered, "I heard papa say he's still alive and he's hiding." "Well then, maybe it was him come back to kill again," Elvin finished.

The spirit of the day the knock was heard hovered like a spell over the children and their schoolhouse. It stayed around until the next May, when the man responsible for their fears was found, tried, and punished by hanging. Many elderly residents of northeast Iowa remember the long search. When the fugitive was finally located and justice was served, the children's fears were finally put to rest.

Mossy Glen Mysteries

Mossy Glen is a beautiful valley fed by three springs, thick with trees, and full of moss-covered stones that gave the valley its name. About 4 or 5 miles west of the small town of Littleport and 8 miles east of Strawberry Point, Mossy Glen is in Lodomillo Township of Clayton County. But despite its serene appearance now, this valley has experienced mysteries and murders since it was first settled in the late 1840s.

The earliest story about the valley concerns a peddler who came to the area selling his wares. One version of the story says an unknown settler or settlers wanted his goods—wanted them so much they were willing to kill for them. Another is that the peddler was killed for the gold he carried, found during the brief Strawberry Point gold strike in about 1858. Legend has it that the peddler was buried at Mossy Glen. There is a cave there, near a stream, and some think his bones lie deep in the cave.

After the peddler's death, strange sounds were heard in the glen and the valley was unusually cool, even in the hottest Iowa summers. John McDonough wrote a poem entitled "Mossy Glen," and in it he refers to the peddler's death: "But his ghost haunts the Glen seeking vengeance/And howls in the blackest midnight."

Another unexplained disappearance in the early days of Mossy Glen was that of a local attorney. His wife had died mysteriously while the family was visiting the area. Rumor was that the husband had arranged for her death. Following his wife's death, the man was plagued by misfortunes, said to be caused by her unhappy spirit.

Early one hazy evening, the attorney was seen driving his buggy out of town and heard to remark he had an appointment at Mossy Glen "to take care of this bad luck." He was never heard from again. Some say his body vanished into one of the many sinkholes that dot the glen.

But the most famous Mossy Glen story is the Shine murder case of 1936. Pearl, an ambitious, red-haired young lady of 27, married Dan Shine, a reclusive 60-year-old backwoods farmer. The new Mrs. Shine, formerly the housekeeper, had been married and divorced twice before. Less than a week after the April 30 wedding, Pearl and the hired hand, not yet 20, filed a new will at the Clayton County Courthouse in Elkader. This new will named Mrs. Shine as the beneficiary and first in line to inherit the 80-acre Shine farm at Mossy Glen should anything happen to Mr. Shine. Within three days, Mr.

Shine's "suicide" was discovered by the Clayton County sheriff and a deputy.

After a thorough investigation, officers determined that Shine had been knocked unconscious and put in the small second-story closet where the body was found. A string had been attached to the shotgun trigger and pulled. He was shot in the head. Medical evidence showed Dan Shine had been killed the same day the new will was filed by Mrs. Shine and the hired hand.

The Shine case received wide coverage in the newspapers. It was also written up in a detective magazine. At one time, 10 people were in jail in connection with the murder, but eventually Mrs. Shine was found guilty of first degree murder and the hired hand of second degree murder. In addition, three others, two of them Mrs. Shine's relatives, were found guilty of being accessories.

Following the murder, children would go to the glen and dare each other to stay after dark. Those few who tried came home quickly, terrified. They talked about the strange, darting shadows in those woods Dan Shine knew so well. Today children still taunt each other about being "'fraidy cats" at the glen and the Shine murder case is still talked about. Whether Dan Shine ever got revenge is not known. Mrs. Shine and the hired hand were paroled in 1952 and chose to live far away from northeast Iowa.

How many spirits haunt Mossy Glen? We know of at least three. But how many more are there? According to John McDonough's poem, these spirits reside at "a wild rocky gorge in the woodland/That is called by the name Mossy Glen."

The Nisse or Hulda?

Some things would happen anyhow, no matter what folks do. That's the way it is. But other things just wouldn't happen unless they were made to happen. In that case, someone is to blame.

Sometimes the blame falls on the nisse. They are the little people living among Norwegians and comparable to leprechauns, the mischievous folk of Irish lore. If you've never met a nisse, you should. In a community such as Decorah, where there are many Norwegians, there are nisse all over the place. Some are real; some are wooden representations of the spirit nisse. You'll see them swinging in the trees or smiling or winking from windows in many homes, even from attic windows.

Because the spirit nisse can do both good and bad things, they are often blamed for what others do. It's as easy to blame a nisse, you see, as it is to blame a ghost. Especially if you're a Norwegian!

Well, sometimes a person just doesn't know who really is at fault, so either a nisse or a ghost can be blamed.

That's what happens at one old farm in Winneshiek County. When bad things happen there to perfectly good people, some folks say, "The nisse did it." Others say, "It had to be Hulda."

Maybe it's both. Maybe they take turns.

Hulda is the ghost who is said to inhabit the house on the old farm. She comes from a long way back. No one would think of turning her out. She probably thinks she belongs there even more than the mortal occupants of the place. She used to live there.

Guests who visit for the first time report a strange feeling while in the house. They say it's as if there is something of the supernatural lurking there. And that's before they've been told about Hulda.

Those who feel at home on the farm have come to accept Hulda, and she stays in the background pretty much. If you know about her, you might acknowledge her presence when you're out there and let yourself absorb the feel of the place and fit in. But if someone new shows up and begins to act really, truly at home, as if to take over, something's sure to happen to set them down a spell.

Take, for example, a number of years ago, when a couple of fellows lived in the house for the summer. The younger brother, least acquainted there at the time, proceeded to pour his Saturday night bath water into the old-fashioned four-legged tub in the room at the top of the stairs. Just as he sat down and reached for the soap, he saw out of the corner of his eye a woman dressed in black moving soundlessly through the next room, from doorway to doorway. Needless to say, he cut his bath short and went looking for the woman. His brother told him, "You've probably just met Hulda. There's no one else around."

Hulda has been responsible for family photos being turned face to the wall or disappearing from their frames entirely. It's one of her little tricks. She seems to have it in for certain people. She lets it be known quite openly, yet she also has a streak of kindness in her. For instance, now and then the cats are treated to the milk from a worker's thermos. Unknown, of course, to the worker. While he's in the field or barn or machine shed, the cats move lazily up to the house and lap up the milk that has just been warmed in the chipped blue enameled pan and set on the porch by the back door. The worker finds his thermos mysteriously empty when he stops for his lunch break. As he munches his herring sandwich, he wonders if the milk was "borrowed" to feed the cats, or to keep the nisse amiable.

Though some items of furniture that once belonged to Hulda have been removed by family members, an old organ was left there. As hard as it is to believe, the organ still works, and whenever the people who own the farm have guests, they encourage any guest so inclined to play it, so as to keep it in good condition. Though it might not play in tune for them, with enough people singing, no one notices. But when there's no one around but the workers, and they approach the house for any reason at all, they are likely to hear the old organ playing as if it were a player piano. One song after another rolls out, each note in perfect tune. Yet no one is in the house. All the searchers can find is a shadow, or a footprint on the stairs—the same stairs on which mysterious footsteps are often heard from other parts of the house. And sometimes the old rocking chair behind the door into the parlor is still rocking after the searchers leave the house.

Probably the most puzzling and distressing incident of all took place last summer, and true to form, it happened to Buck Wilson, the newest worker. He stepped into the house just after dark to pick up some keys he'd left there in the afternoon. No one was home at the time, but he knew just where to find them. He didn't need a light. All he had to do was step up to the small table in the middle of the first room and pick them up.

But when he did, he was suddenly plunged downward through the cistern cover in the floor. He fell directly into the cold water below. Now, that bordered on the tragic. There was no ladder in the cistern. None had been needed since the cover was rebuilt, because the table was always right over the spot. But fortunately for Buck, his friend John Skaim had gone out to work that day, too, and was waiting in his van, ready to leave. He'd been watching the sky and recognizing all the signs of an approaching thunderstorm. When he thought about how long he'd been waiting, John got a little impatient with "this new help" and went up to the porch to find out what was happening. He found out. Buck called to him from down in the cistern. John could hardly hear him over the increasing howl of the wind. He thought of Hulda and wondered what she was up to. When he went on in, he saw Buck's predicament and almost laughed. He got a ladder and a light and rescued his friend.

Buck asked John, "Why on earth didn't you tell me you moved that table?"

"What table?"

"The one you told me to always keep over the cistern cover."

"What are you talking about? I sure didn't move it. Did you have a light on?"

"No. I didn't think I needed one. Half the time, the lights go out around here anyway, even when I have 'em turned on! But the table was moved, and I fell into a trap. I guess If you didn't move it, I wonder who did?"

On the way down the lane, Buck, still shaking and even more violently now as the truth dawned on him, blurted out, "John, that must have been Hulda!"

John answered him easily even as a great horned owl swooped down and buzzed the van's windshield. "You finally realize I didn't have a thing to do with it. Buck, you were just being initiated into the crew out there. It has happened to all of us, at one time or another. You might have expected either the nisse or the ghost to be watching for you!"

One Family's Sense of Spirit

There are individuals who have dealt with the phenomenon of strange happenings over a period of years. The resulting effect, or perhaps the cause, is a special sensitivity to spirits or ghosts. That sensitivity somehow becomes an element in the life of the person. It seems that several members of a family may also possess the sensitivity and be affected by it. One family's experiences, as told by the mother, spread over the years from 1954 to the present.

The mother, Colleen, said that when she was about 12, she had the same scary dream several times, just two or three weeks apart. She always woke up before it was over. At the time, she lived in her parents' home about three-quarters of a mile west of McGregor.

A band of nomads camping farther west, toward Giard, sometimes came by their house on the way into town. Most people around there had heard of them and had seen them occasionally, as had Colleen and her family.

One of the nomads appeared in her recurring dream. He'd be slowly walking down the road and around the bend about two houses west, approaching the house where Colleen lived. In each dream, Colleen would see that in one hand he held a knife with a long, shiny blade. She would always wake up then, before he came any nearer.

After several dreams like that, on a very real Saturday afternoon, the phone rang. Colleen's mother answered it. It was a neighbor screaming hysterically, "Lock your doors. A nomad with a knife just threatened me and he's headed your way."

"Mother told me," Colleen said, "to quickly go out on the porch and lock the door. I just stood there frozen. It was an enclosed porch with windows all across the front and sides. My mother went out there, and she had to crawl on her hands and knees beneath eight porch windows. She got there just in time to lock the door before he started rattling it to get in. Then, while he stood there looking in, Mother crouched behind the lower, solid part of the door. She didn't have time to get back in the house unseen.

"Finally, when I saw her predicament, I could move. My sisters and I knew we had to help her to protect our family. We ran and locked the other doors before he got to them. He tried each one. He didn't get in, though. And after that real experience, I never had that same dream again.

"But other things started happening to me, and I wondered if the dreams had awakened a special awareness in me of the unusual.

"By 1967 I had married and we had started our own family. We lived in a three-bedroom house in a town in Winneshiek County. Amy was our youngest at the time. She was about 3 and had a bedroom all to herself, across from ours. No one else in the family noticed anything unusual, but I could hardly breathe in her bedroom, near the closet. I could feel a presence there, and it was cold.

"Trying to get rid of the feeling, I painted Amy's closet and papered her room in happy colors. It made no difference. During the night, she often woke up crying. I would jump up and go to her room, but I could never go past her doorway. Something always stopped me. I would call, then, for her to come to me, and she would.

"One very early morning, I woke up hearing a child crying outside. I jumped up and ran downstairs within two seconds. I unlocked the door and went out to Amy, who stood there facing the house and crying. She was too short to reach the lock, so I can't explain how she got outside when the door was locked. It was really weird!

"At that time, our good friends had a hypnotist staying with them. Because of my reactions to strange phenomena, I had also met him. One evening, under hypnosis, he asked me to try to communicate with the ghost in our house. Out of that experience, the following explanation came to me.

"The ghost was a woman who had died, leaving her older sister all alone. She had stayed in the house, as a ghost, to protect her sister. When the older sister moved out, the spirit stayed around and spread her mantle of protection over Amy.

"The hypnotist suggested that I confront our ghost. I did. Still under hypnosis, I thanked her. I said to her, 'Your sister has moved away, and so she doesn't need you here anymore. She has found peace wherever she is. As for our family, we're all OK and we don't need your protection. Please leave us alone and go and find your peace too.' The next day brought a great change in the atmosphere in that house. It was as if someone had opened a window and let the fresh air in. The ghost was gone. After that, Amy never again woke up crying during the night."

Then Colleen went on to another incident. She said, "The next year, my grandfather died. He was in his 90s. He had been healthy to the last and had lived a good life.

"We were all at Monona for the funeral. During the services, I began to wonder if I could communicate with his spirit. I sort of thought-spoke, 'If you can hear me, Grandpa, show me some sign.' Just then, the lamp behind me went out. I never did tell that one to anyone before. It definitely startled me then, but I kind of forgot about it until now.

"Not long after that, things started happening that affected others in the family. In 1973, we moved into an apartment house we owned. We already had a tenant living upstairs, so we moved into the downstairs apartment. There was nothing unusual about the house itself, and I had no bad feelings about the apartments. But out in the backyard, there was another house, a smaller one, with one room up and one down, that we thought we could use for storage. There was already some furniture out there, in the upper room, when we moved into the apartment in the front house. We found an old cot and a rocking chair there. The steps were narrow and steep, so we wondered if someone had moved the furniture up and in through the window and just didn't want to take it down again. Our girls thought the little house would make a good place to play. They took their Barbie dolls and houses out there, and it went all right until dark. Then they would run back into the main house. Whenever I went out to see what had scared them, I would feel as if a bad spirit was there. When I listened to my feelings, I thought someone had met with a tragic death in that house.

"I felt that I had to do something about it, if we were going to keep on living in the apartment. I went to the Decorah Public Library and checked out a book on hex signs. I made one then, to hang inside the 'playhouse.' After that, I felt more comfortable about it. But once, the girls wanted to have a slumber party out there. They went to a lot of work to get it ready and take their blankets and pillows and all that out; but as soon as it got dark, they hurried back into the house with us, where they felt safer.

"Before our upstairs apartment tenant moved out, she told me a little about that house in the back. She said that a long, long time ago, a previous landlord had shot himself in it. His spirit must have hung around through the time we lived there. All those years we stayed, I had bad feelings whenever I was in the house in back.

"Strange feelings kept on coming to me too. I was visiting relatives in St. Louis once. In different rooms in their house, I felt different vibrations. When I stood looking out the front window at the other houses and yards in the block, I sensed that someone had once stood there and watched a person drown. I told my aunt about it, and she said it was true. Before the other houses were built, there was a lake out in front of the house my aunt was living in. A woman no longer in the area had actually stood at that same window once and watched her son's boat capsize on the lake. He drowned before anyone could get help.

"Our family moved again, a little later. We have a spirit living with us now, in our present home. Our oldest daughter, Tina, was the first to see her. She woke up one night and saw a woman standing in the doorway of her bedroom. That was back in about 1979. Tina's married now and lives in another state, but a couple of years ago I woke up one night and saw a woman standing in the same doorway.

"My husband and our other daughter, Debbie, have both heard her footsteps on the stairs at night. On two occasions, Debbie's music box that's been broken for years started playing during the night, and Debbie felt the presence of someone in her room while it was playing. She's 18 now, and a couple of times lately, Deb woke up screaming, she was so sure someone was in her room other than her family.

"So far, this spirit seems to be harmless, so we haven't confronted her or put up a hex sign. But the more I think about it, the more I wonder how long our family will be having such unusual things happening. Even Amy, after she moved into a new apartment in another state, has heard unexplainable sounds, and strange things have been happening to her TV.

"Life would definitely lack something if this sense of spirit in our family ever came to an end! I just hope that all the spirits that visit us will be harmless, or that if they are hard to live with, we'll be able to confront them or deal with them to everyone's satisfaction."

"Please Excuse Us, Augie"

Heidi was a resident assistant (R.A. for short) in Noehren Hall on the University of Northern Iowa campus in Cedar Falls. As R.A., she talked with many of the residents of Noehren as well as other dorms. They came to her with their questions and problems. They also came with stories they heard from friends. The stories and conversations often lasted far into the night.

The stories Heidi heard most often in her last term as R.A. centered around a man who was seen several times walking around in the corridors at Lawther Hall. He definitely wasn't a close friend of any of the current students, according to the girls who spoke about him. In fact, he hardly seemed to fit into the place or times. The girls asked Heidi if they ought to report this stranger to campus security. Heidi felt a need to find out more about him first.

Heidi had gone over to Lawther one evening earlier that fall, before the hall opened for the semester. She was helping Cindy and Stacey decorate a large bulletin board to have it ready for opening. As they mulled through a box of letters of all shapes and sizes, looking for the right ones, they saw a man walk by. He was wearing what seemed in one quick glance to be a uniform. The girls knew there shouldn't have been anyone else in the dorm at the time, especially at night—unless he was a repairman or custodian—so, all together, the three followed him. He went up the dark, steep stairs at the end of the hall, where he selected a key from a ring of keys looped in his belt and unlocked the door. He disappeared at that moment. They saw no one in the attic or anywhere near the stairs, and they found the door at the other end of the attic locked.

A bit shaken, they went back to their bulletin board project to finish it. That night they all went over to Heidi's room at Noehren to sleep on mattresses gathered from nearby rooms.

A couple of months later, after classes started and everything was rolling along routinely, Heidi offered to help the Lawther R.A.s again. They had to get ready for a special event held every year at Halloween. It had become a tradition to decorate the Lawther attic for a fun, spooky evening. Students from other dorms were welcome.

This was about the twelfth time the event had been held, according to what the R.A.s were told. Their responsibility was to prepare the attic so that all who came could walk down its long, dark hall; hear a creaky door suddenly slam shut; or hear a click of a lock in the door at the far end of the attic followed by a haunting, drawn-out laugh or a terrified scream. All of it was intended, of course, to give the impression that a ghost or ghosts haunted the attic.

Just before the Halloween event, several residents of Bordeaux house in Lawther laughed about the new arrangement on the bulletin board near the kitchen door. It referred, in part, to the "scary, spooky, bone-chilling night" to be held in the attic. They didn't think their bones would be chilled by it. But an hour later, when they came out of the kitchen, they saw that the letters had been rearranged to read "Augie will return to haunt Bordeaux house."

The girls didn't recognize the name Augie in connection with anyone they knew, and no one else was around at the time. They had no idea who had changed the message.

After that happened, there was more talk about unexplainable incidents and the possibility of real ghosts "living" in the attic or anywhere else in the dorm.

In those late-night talk sessions, both at Lawther and at Noehren, other stories came to light. Barb, a Lawther resident, was sleeping in her own room one night. She thought she heard her roommate Krista come in, run the faucets, and climb into her top bunk. During the rest of the night, Barb woke up several more times to the sounds of running water and the creaking of the bunk above hers. In the morning, when she asked Krista why she was up so many times, Krista said, "I wasn't. I stayed over in Noehren with Susan. I just came in while you were in the shower."

Shelley, another Lawther resident, reported seeing a strange "black aura" floating around in her room. She said the shape hovered over her study lamp, moved around a little, and then was gone. She said, "It scared me. I didn't know what it was, and I still don't."

Cindy said she had often felt as if she was being watched by someone other than her roommate or friends, but as R.A. she couldn't let it upset her. She just thought other girls were hanging around, trying to decide whether to bother her with their problems.

Sometimes students heard noises at night, during quiet hours, especially in the time of year when late fall begins to change to nearly winter. Sometimes all was quiet, with many students gone to the library or a concert or play for the evening. When they returned, they would find pages turned, books moved, notebooks closed. During the night some reported that their covers were sometimes pulled off.

Barb told Heidi about a cold area in front of that bulletin board in Bordeaux house. She thought it was the spot where Augie went in and out of the attic, and maybe still does.

Shelley said, "And that's the exact same spot the weird black aura disappeared, when it left my room!"

Others told of lights being on in the attic when no one was allowed to be up there, or of loud thumps on the ceiling of the third-floor, or of sounds of furniture being moved above the third-floor rooms. There were many nights scary enough to send all the girls from that floor down into rooms on the first or second floors for the rest of the night.

After a number of stories came to light, Cindy and Stacey decided to get to the bottom of it. Heidi offered to help. At the Donald O. Rod library, the archivist helped them locate copies of *The Northern Iowan* from the past few years. They realized that browsing through so many copies would take more time than they had, so they decided to start with some late-October issues.

They found there had been similar occurrences over a period of at least 10 years. They also learned that the Lawther Hall Halloween event had been held in "Augie's Attic" for several years. The news editors and staff writers spoke openly of "Augie's Attic."

Several stories agreed as to who Augie was: a soldier who died in the attic of Lawther when the building was used as an infirmary during World War I. Since then, the girls concluded, "His ghost now lives in the attic and crawl spaces up there, as well as in other top floors of Lawther!"

During World War I, Augie might have been one of many victims of tuberculosis. On the other hand, maybe Augie wasn't in the infirmary on account of his own illness. An article in *The Northern Iowan* suggested that he was possibly visiting his girlfriend who was sick in the infirmary, took sick himself, and died in the attic.

However it happened, Augie apparently died there and has lingered ever since. He has been seen walking the halls, climbing the stairs, unlocking doors, and roaming in and out of rooms on the upper floors of Lawther.

Some residents reported that Augie wore a pin-striped suit when they saw him. Others said he was wearing an old army uniform. So he could have been a soldier, or he could have been a boyfriend who dressed up "spiffy" to visit his girl.

Thoughtful, practical Heidi told the girls, "Maybe we'd better ask Augie if he minds if we invade his quarters to decorate his attic and hold this event. I know it's eerie and unexplainable, but all the stories

I've heard lead me to one conclusion: Augie's ghost lives in the attic of Lawther Hall, so it's only right to call it 'Augie's Attic' and to ask Augie to forgive us for disrupting his life."

Porter House Ghosties

Visitors to the redbrick Victorian Porter House Museum on West Broadway in Decorah often experience an indescribable feeling as they ascend the lovely stairway to the second floor. They feel a presence of some kind there, its true nature unknown to them. Others, even members of the current board of directors, feel insecure when they have an errand at the house. They admit they would rather not go in alone.

But the house did not frighten the four children of Harriet Bennett Norton. They had come to the Ellsworth mansion in 1877 when their mother married Dighton (D.B.) Ellsworth a year after his first wife, Amanda, died. In fact, the four loved to play in the house.

Whenever D.B. and Harriet entertained in the parlor, Harriet's children were free to wander through the rest of the house. Sometimes they went down the back stairway, into the kitchen and pantry. While the servants were occupied with feeding the guests, the children stole from the kitchen down to the basement and came up into the backyard by way of the outside cellar steps. Their favorite place, though, was the tower.

It took some doing, but when Harriet's four children and their stepfather's two young grandchildren were all together at holiday time they used every chance to go up there. As soon as Harriet left the house, they gathered at the top of the elegant, curved stairway with its polished walnut balustrade. Pulling on their heaviest sweaters, they tiptoed through the storeroom and proceeded as usual up the narrower stairs to the tower room. Martin usually cleared the cobwebs away with an old broom. Lauraette often carried a lighted candle. George would help his stepsister Florence's two small children, hardly able to climb the stairs themselves yet. Little Orinda (the others called her Rennie) squeezed up through the trapdoor square last, dragging her old doll with her. The tower or belvedere was not a major part of the structure, but it was impressive. Some said the windows on all four sides of the tower gave the house an airy and somewhat pretentious look.

Whatever its purpose, the six youngsters accepted the challenge it presented. To them, it was the most interesting part of the house. They loved to look out over the town and imagine what it was like before their stepfather built the house in 1867 and before other early settlers like the Days, the Bucknells, the Landers, the Painters, and Mrs. Hughes built their homes nearby.

During the winter of 1878–79, D.B. Ellsworth still operated a dry goods business down at the bottom of the hill, and gifts as well as supplies could be bought there. On a late December afternoon, when Harriet left the house to enlist her husband's help with the

Christmas purchases, the servants were busy in the kitchen, making crumpets and plum pudding and other delicacies that graced the holiday tables of the English families in the community. Preparing those foods required the complete attention of the servants, and so the children once again made use of the chance to go up to the tower.

Once there, Lauraette set the candle on a ledge where its light reflected off the windows and bounced back and forth with the air currents from the stairs. It was a rule that the last one up had to leave the door at the bottom open, for the dim light that came up from the storeroom.

Because it was late afternoon in December and it was starting to snow, the tower was brightened only by the wavering, eerie light from the candle. That, along with the frost settling on the cold windows from the breathing of six children in the small space, resulted in a strange effect to anyone who chanced to look up from outside.

As Etta (Lauraette liked it when the others shortened her name) wiped a window clear so she could see out, she thought she saw someone waving to her. She was looking north across the street and west toward the octagon house at the other end of the block. When she was sure someone was there, she told the others. They thought they, too, could see someone on the lookout at the top of the other house. It looked like a man moving along heavily, unsteadily. At first, because of the distance between the houses and the bothersome frosting up of the tower windows, the figure looked more spirit-like than human. But when it waved its arms around, it looked much like a person about to fall over the railing.

George asked, "But who could be out there in the cold? It doesn't even look like he has on a shirt or a coat."

Martin said, "I wonder if he wants us to help him down."

They wiped their hands back and forth on the cold windows again, and once more they saw someone waving back, even more frantically, it seemed.

Just as the children planned to leave their haunt and go across the street to help, they heard stomping downstairs and knew their parents would be in the front entrance, taking off their snowy boots and wraps. The six of them quickly wriggled one by one through the opening in the floor, worked their way cautiously down the steps, stowed the candle and broom at the bottom, and reminded Rennie to close the door before they met Mr. and Mrs. Ellsworth's inquisitive glances directed up toward them.

The adults thought they saw the shining eyes and bright cheeks of six darling youngsters all aglow with the excitement of the season and with curiosity about the queerly shaped bundles poking out in all directions from the shoppers' arms and coat pockets. Little did they know that the children had just spent another thrilling hour in the tower room that they couldn't mention for fear they might be scolded.

The children didn't reveal their secret until many years later, when it became known that an early occupant of the octagon house was frequently seen by others, too, in a red-nosed and very unsteady condition, out on the high lookout. Whenever that happened, it is said it took several men to go up there and persuade him to come back inside. He probably thought the children were waving to him that December afternoon, and they thought he was signaling for help. If he wasn't, they thought he was going to need it anyway, but they had to spend the rest of the evening hoping he got down safely without them. And Rennie had to go to sleep without her doll. She had forgotten to pick it up when they all started down in a hurry.

It is said there are bats in the belvedere now. Perhaps there are also ghosts of the people who lived there so long ago.

Perhaps Harriet's children sent their spirits back to haunt the dark stairway and the tower. Passersby sometimes think they see children waving from the frost-patterned windows.

Any house that is 120 years old is likely to boast its ghosts. The Ellsworth-Porter House, now the Porter House Museum, is one of those. But the ghosts are of a playful nature. That is why they are referred to as the Porter House ghosties.

The Skeleton's Hand

The house was in National, in the Garnavillo area, which boasts of perhaps the richest, blackest land in Clayton County. Once a thriving community, National is now only a small gathering of houses.

But the house did—maybe still does—exist. Or so a local man says his grandfather, now dead, told him. His grandfather was a great storyteller, and this story, which happened about 1910, was one he swore was true.

The elegant, two-story, brick home and the land had been owned by a doctor before the Hans Neyerman family bought the farm. The doctor had a good practice and was by all accounts an excellent medical man. He was also a bit eccentric. Because there were few laws regarding burials then, the bodies of the poor and of criminals who died were often used by the medical profession to learn about the human body and its ailments. Somehow, during his years of medical practice, the doctor had obtained a skeleton that he insisted was that of a famous criminal. He kept this ghoulish item in an upstairs bedroom closet and frequently brought it out for his guests to view, whether they wanted to or not. He would only laugh when they cringed, saying, "It's only the live ones you have to worry about!"

Hans and his family—wife, two boys, and three girls—bought the farm in late 1909. The doctor's health was declining and by spring, when the Neyermans were to move in, the doctor had died. The doctor's wife took the lovely furniture and the thick velvet drapes from the arched windows, but she left the skeleton. She had always hated it, she told Hans, and he was welcome to it.

Hans did not really want the skeleton either, but he had much to do and he could not bury the skeleton when the ground was still frozen. But he assured his wife, Augusta, that he would move it as soon as spring came. He would give the skeleton a decent burial in the small private plot on the farm.

The children at first would not go near the room at the top of the stairs. This bedroom was used as a storeroom. But, gradually, the children started to peek inside, then quickly retreat. They began to stay a little longer until they were all boldly entering the room (though only in the daytime) and playing there. All except Marie, the youngest. She was 7 and did not like the bedroom or the closet or anything in the "scare room." In the evenings, the children would complain the room was too chilly and dark to play in, even though it was lit with candles as the other rooms were.

The family got used to the house and, despite Hans's promises, he did not get the skeleton removed and buried. Marie had a birthday that June and wanted to have a party. Hans thought a party an extravagance, but he had a soft spot for his youngest and finally consented, promising her he would have the skeleton out before her birthday in two weeks. However, the day before the party, it rained hard and Hans couldn't bury the skeleton.

Eight little boys and girls arrived in their parents' buggies and wagons, the girls in long dresses and the boys in knickers. First to arrive was Karine, a fair-skinned girl with blond, straight hair. She was Marie's best friend. Karine's parents were Norwegian, unusual in this solid German community, and Karine was teased because of her Scandinavian accent. But today she was very happy because her mother had let her wear a special outfit. She had on a red-and-white Norwegian costume, hand-embroidered by her grandmother. Marie thought the outfit was beautiful.

After eating cake, the children played games. Never having been in the house before, they wanted to play hide and seek so they could explore this fancy home. They had also heard about the skeleton from their parents, though Marie would never talk about it.

Reluctantly, Augusta gave permission—if they were careful—and they were not to go upstairs. Marie started the game and, several turns later, she was "it" again. Even though she was not supposed to, Karine's curiosity got the better of her and she snuck up the oak staircase. She crouched down to peer at Marie through the railing. When Marie got to "eight," Karine slipped into the first room she saw, at the top of the stairs. The door was slightly ajar. Despite the fact that it was June, the day had become dark; storm clouds were returning. By now, Karine could hear Marie saying "10!"

In the gloomy room, Karine could see a small bed against the opposite wall. A dresser was on her left and a rag rug covered the shiny wood floor. Karine could just make out a door near the foot of the bed. As she started toward this door, thunder boomed and she jumped back. She remembered seeing a lighted candle on a table in the hallway. She ducked back out, took the candle, and set it on the dresser in the room. The soft glow made her feel better. Taking off her red cap, she set it carefully on the dresser and walked towards the closet door.

By this time, Marie had found all the other children and, giving up, hollered for Karine to come out. But Karine did not come. They quickly searched the downstairs and decided to ask Mrs. Neyerman. Augusta started to look but suddenly spied the light under the closet door at the top of the stairs just as Karine screamed. Augusta ran up the steps, Marie and the other children following. As they opened the door, they saw Karine, white and shaking, stagger out of the closet and collapse.

Augusta rushed to her and lifted up her head, instructing one of the boys to get Hans and to tell him to get a doctor.

"He grabbed me, he grabbed me. He wouldn't let go," Karine whispered. Her eyes rolled back and she went limp. "Who?" asked Augusta, shaking the small body gently.

"Him, Mommy," said Marie, pointing to the closet. And there was the skeleton, long blond strands of hair in its right hand.

By the time the doctor arrived, Karine had died. The doctor said she died of heart failure. He thought she may have had a weak heart and the shock of the incident killed her. Hans removed the skeleton and buried it in an unmarked grave. Augusta locked the door to the closet and to the room. The family never used the room again.

The man who told this story does not recall the precise spot his grandfather said the house stood. The house may still be there, doors locked.

They've Always Been With Us

Inga has been seeing ghosts or spirits since the day she moved to the old farmhouse in the northeast Iowa countryside as a new bride in 1979. That very first night, surrounded by wedding gifts, she glanced outside and saw a man standing in the yard, wearing a long black coat. A few moments later, she saw the same man on the other side of the yard. Her husband had gone to town to get a few more things and they didn't even have curtains on the windows. Inga was so terrified that she hurriedly opened up gifts until she found a set of knives and sat in the middle of the gifts, clutching a knife. When she told her husband, he suggested she was just overly tired. She did her best to forget about the episode.

Months later, though, she saw a glimpse of the same man going up the stairs from the kitchen and later from a bedroom to the attic. She was still scared, but curious. During the times she saw the man, he did not seem to emanate evil and she did not feel threatened. Instead, he just seemed to be walking around. She never saw his face, for he wore the long black coat and a black hat. Often she would hear someone come in and sit down on a chair in the kitchen, but after getting up and checking, she found no one there. One time she heard snoring next to her in bed, although her husband was not in bed with her. Her daughters had also heard the sounds of someone breathing loudly.

After checking with neighbors, she found out that a man had died of a stroke in the yard on the farm. His family was a bit peculiar and, while waiting for the doctor, they draped a long black coat over him and left him in the yard. Inga also found out this was just one of many stories about her new home.

The family that had lived in the home before Inga and her family had moved from another small salt-box-type home and built this one. Although the family had five children, none of them married and they all lived together in the house. One brother died of the flu in his twenties. Inga said they found a letter in the attic from the young man, and it was obvious he knew he was going to die. She does not know what happened to the letter. Another brother was the one who died of a stroke on the lawn. Then there was the sister who was at the well or cistern getting water when she fell in and drowned. However, dark rumors also suggest that she had jumped into the well.

About 10 years after her marriage, Inga saw a young girl, about 5 or 6 years old. She remembers vividly the first time she saw the little girl. Inga was sitting in the dining room one cold Saturday in January, doing book work. She looked up and saw a small girl, skipping into the room from the kitchen. The girl paused and looked at Inga and Inga looked back. To this day, Inga remembers the little girl was wearing a dusky blue dress with white flowers, and she wore high-top boots. Her long, light-brown hair fell around her shoulders and she had a big bow in her hair to match her dress. She suddenly skipped away and was gone. A different time, Inga heard giggles and girlish laughter from the house when her own daughters were not home. Later on, the youngest daughter, 6 at the time, came to her mother and said a girl had just come skipping into the dining room and looked at her. Another time a different daughter saw a little girl kneeling in front of the stuffed bear the family kept in the upstairs hallway.

About a year ago, the upstairs toilet stopped working. One day it was functioning and the next day it wasn't. A plumber paid a visit and after checking it out, he wanted to know why they had removed all the plumbing parts from the tank. The family was astonished when the plumber lifted the tank cover: the inside was completely empty.

At times, Inga would put her car keys in the place where she always kept them, and the next day they would be gone. They might be in a cupboard or hidden behind a canister. Another time Inga put down her makeup bag and stepped out of the room. When she came back, it was gone. She went downstairs to see if it was there, and when she returned upstairs the bag was right where it should have been. A hairbrush and curling iron disappeared and reappeared too. Were these tricks played by the little girl?

When an elderly neighbor showed Inga a confirmation picture of the woman who had drowned in the well, Inga recognized the girl in the picture as her ghostly visitor, even though the confirmation picture showed a girl of 13 or 14.

Despite the fact that the family does not feel the spirits are malevolent, none of the children will stay in the house alone and Inga feels uneasy by herself. Her husband has never seen any of these ghostly visitors, and is somewhat skeptical of them, despite the stories from his wife and daughters. Inga feels he does not see the apparitions because he does not let himself see them. The family does not plan on moving from their scenic northeast Iowa farm, with its rolling hills and valleys, but Inga and her daughters are always on the lookout for any ghosts.

Tricked by a Troll

Some people say they have seen or sensed the presence of ghosts. And many people of Scandinavian descent say they have seen or felt the presence of trolls—troublesome beings. Trolls live in all of northeast Iowa, but most of the stories about these Norwegian imports center around Decorah.

There are several kinds of trolls. Water trolls live in the Upper Iowa River and in numerous creeks and streams. Bridge trolls live under College Drive Bridge or the Tavener Bridge near Pulpit Rock. Large wood trolls and rock trolls with their square, flat heads live in the woods and parks—Palisades Park, Dunning's Spring, Phelps Park, and Malanaphy Springs, to name a few. The trolls may live anywhere, but their headquarters is Ice Cave, just north of Decorah.

All trolls are ugly, but people say the water trolls, with their light-green, slippery, slimy hair are the ugliest. They spend most of their time underwater, with only their hair floating on the surface. Occasionally, their bulging, dark eyes can be seen peeping out from the water.

Our story concerns Lars Larson and his encounter with these mischievous creatures. One day Lars decided he wanted to go fishing. He probably should have gone to work, but it was a clear, sunny summer day. So instead he took his fishing pole and tackle box and headed for a new, secret fishing spot on a small stream that fed into the Upper Iowa. He had found the spot over a month ago, but this would be his first chance to fish it.

Lars parked his car on the road and started the long walk to the creek. While trying to avoid a wall of tall weeds, he brushed by a patch of gooseberry bushes and ripped a hole in his pants. Then he tripped not once but twice over large rocks he did not remember from his first visit.

When Lars reached the creek, he baited his hook and fished from a small, wooden bridge. To the right was a marshy area with cattails and assorted water-loving weeds. Lars was sure there were fish just waiting to be caught in this secret spot. No sooner had he thrown his line in than he felt a tug. Pulling hard, he found a rusty tin can on the end of the line. Lars was removing the tin can when he saw the cattails on his right whipping back and forth. He studied the area. The movement stopped. Just weeds—or had he seen something else? Wondering, he baited his hook again and settled back. The sun was high and hot now, and he was getting drowsy. A powerful jerk pulled the pole almost out of his hands. Struggling to hold on, Lars braced his feet against the side of the bridge and leaned back. But the bridge was old and shaky, and Lars was yanked through the rotted railings and off the bridge.

He landed in a deep pocket in the stream and fought to get to the surface. He could see what looked like light-green weeds all around him, and he was tangled up in them. Lars felt as though the weeds were really 1,000 fingers, pulling him down. At last he struggled free and stood upright in the shallow part of the creek. Lars heard a laugh and turned around to see two black, fish-like eyes duck under the water. The green seaweed moved rapidly down the stream, with his line and pole attached.

Lars was shaking, and not just from the cold water. He went home immediately. Lars vowed he would never skip work again to go fishing. Only he and the water troll knew the reason why.

Why Does the Angel Cry?

Some unusual things have happened at the cemetery out at Parker's Grove, along a graveled country road north and east of Shellsburg and not very far from town.

One of the unusual incidents happened the night Deanna and her friends went out to the cemetery. First they wandered around for a while, just sensing the somber mood of the burial grounds. The peaceful quiet impressed all of them. Then they noticed how varied the tombstones were in size and shape and age. They found that most of the older ones stood tall, and many of those were gray or white and dull and worn. Some of them had been reset on their bases. Others had broken corners or tops that had toppled off.

As dusk deepened into evening, someone noticed that those tall markers made shadows as varied as their shapes. On some of the very old ones, the lettering was so worn down that it was hardly visible; on others, lichens had grown to obliterate parts of the information. It was hard to trace the old ones to read the names and dates. As their fingers moved lightly over them, one of Deanna's friends said, "This must be a lot like how the blind read Braille."

Many of the more recent markers were either very tall or quite low. Some of the large ones marked a family plot, and smaller ones around them marked individual family members' graves. Some of those newer ones were more colorful and even sparkly. Names and dates on most of those were easy to read.

As she read some of the names out loud, one of the girls noticed that a few markers had birth dates from as early as 1865 and 1878, and she found one marked "b. 1885." But the death dates had not been recorded on those tombstones. When she mentioned that to the others, someone jokingly said, "They must be very old—too old, in fact, to still be living!"

Someone else said, "Gee, do you suppose they died but were never buried? Or maybe..."

Deanna interrupted that thought. She said, "I know what you were thinking. If they are still around, they'd have to be ghosts by now! Hey, you guys, we'd better be getting back to town. It's getting darkish and spooky out here and, besides, my tennies are soaked with dew."

Just then, Deanna came upon a marker shaped like an angel. That didn't scare her as much as the thought of ghosts roaming around among the tombstones or floating out from behind the next tall ones. While she was thinking about how pleasant and comforting it would be to have a friendly angel on a tombstone—maybe on her own someday—Deanna reached up and caressed the angel's face. It felt smooth, a little warm, and unexpectedly damp. She reached a little higher and rested her fingertips lightly and briefly just below the angel's eyes. Suddenly she jumped away and started running toward the car.

On the way to town, one of the others asked Deanna why she was in such a hurry to leave.

As soon as she caught her breath, Deanna answered, "Well, it was getting darker all the time, for being where we were. And we were talking about ghosts too. But the scariest thing was when I reached up to the angel's eyes. They were wet."

"Oh, come on! Your hands must have been damp!"

"But they weren't. And I'm sure I felt tears coming from her eyes. It wasn't dew, either. I had to lean on the angel to reach her face, and the rest of her was dry."

"Well, did that scare you?"

"Not just that. I'd been thinking about how comforting it could be to know an angel would be on my tombstone someday, to watch over me and keep me company. Then when I felt the tears, it struck me—it was more as if the angel wanted to be comforted."

Another girl said, "I've heard about that angel before, but I'd almost forgotten about it. Someone told me once that a lot of people have touched it, and the eyes and face felt wet, as if the angel was crying. That must be why they call her 'The Crying Angel.' Because of the tears. I think they say that grave is where a girl about our age was buried, long ago, but you can't read the stuff on the marker anymore."

But Deanna wonders if the crying angel marks the burial place of a girl her age who, for some reason unknown to others, was very unhappy when she died. And now that she has thought about it some more, she thinks the tears are a sign of the dead girl's lasting unhappiness. And since a monument can't cry, Deanna is a lot closer to believing in ghosts. Especially sad ghosts.

About the Authors

Ruth D. Hein grew up in Van Horne, Iowa, and was the middle child in a ghost-free Lutheran parsonage. With a masters degree from the University of Northern Iowa, she taught high school English as well as creative writing for 28 years, 21 of those in Decorah. Ruth lived near Worthington, Minnesota, where she collected ghost stories and wrote the historical column for the *Worthington Daily Globe* for 14 years. She passed away in 2011.

Vicky L. Hinsenbrock's German relatives loved to tell stories of the unexpected happenings when she was growing up in northeast Iowa. A graduate of Iowa State University with a major in animal science, she works for the USDA. She and her husband live in an old Victorian house in the country. No known ghosts inhabit their home.